Dear R...

In December ... ...unt Hood in Oregon. The story captured media attention as rescuers struggled against weather conditions to find t...m.

...ing to learn more about their fate, I stumbled across ...on-line climbing forum where rescuers were posting ...t the search and rescue (SAR) operation. Sadly, the ...bers perished, but the courage of the men and women ...he mountain rescue units inspired and intrigued me. I ...w I had to write this book.

...e problem. I knew nothing about climbing. My husband climbed before we married, and he wanted to climb ...in, but I didn't want him anywhere near Mount Hood's ...mmit. I decided not to ask him for help. Lucky for me, ...e wasn't offended. Through the internet I met climbers—some members of mountain rescue units—who not ...ly helped me with my research, but became friends. T...e more I learned, the less I had to fear about climbing. I ...ven gave my husband a guided trip up Mount Hood as ...ift for our twelfth anniversary. He reached the summit d...ring a climb in May 2007 and loved every minute of it.

M...y curiosity about climbing grew. Though I'm scared of h...ights, I took a class at a local rock gym for some hands-o... research and discovered I loved climbing! I've been climbing ever since.

I...ve written several books, but not one has changed my life t...e way RESCUED BY THE MAGIC OF CHRISTMAS ...d. For those who helped me discover a new passion to ...rsue, all I can say is thank you and climb on!

...elissa

With a degree in mechanical engineering from Stanford University, the last thing **Melissa McClone** ever thought she would be doing was writing romance novels. But analysing engines for a major US airline just couldn't compete with her 'happily-ever-afters'. When she isn't writing, caring for her three young children or doing laundry, Melissa loves to curl up on the couch with a cup of tea, her cats and a good book. She enjoys watching home decorating shows to get ideas for her house—a 1939 cottage that is *slowly* being renovated. Melissa lives in Lake Oswego, Oregon, with her own real-life hero husband, two daughters, a son, two loveable but oh-so-spoiled indoor cats and a no-longer-stray outdoor kitty that decided to call the garage home. Melissa loves to hear from her readers. You can write to her at PO Box 63, Lake Oswego, OR 97034, USA, or contact her via her website: www.melissamcclone.com

RESCUED BY THE MAGIC OF CHRISTMAS

BY
MELISSA McCLONE

MILLS & BOON

Pure reading pleasure™

First published in Great Britain 2008
Harlequin Mills & Boon Limited,
Eton House, 18-24 Paradise Road, Richmond, Surrey TW9 1SR

© Melissa Martinez McClone 2008

ISBN: 978 0 263 86552 3

Set in Times Roman 13 on 14½ pt
02-1108-45620

Printed and bound in Spain
by Litografia Rosés, S.A., Barcelona

Melissa McClone on RESCUED BY THE
MAGIC OF CHRISTMAS:

'*Christmas time is about love and affirming life. My youngest child was due in January, and I drew upon my own experiences for writing Hannah. Like her, I prepared endless lists, hoping to make the holiday the "best ever" for my toddler and preschooler while preparing for the new arrival. Unlike me, Hannah didn't have things go quite as planned, but what better way to celebrate this special season than with the birth of a child?*'

Recent titles by the same author:

WIN, LOSE…OR WED!
MARRIAGE FOR BABY
PLAIN JANE'S PRINCE CHARMING

For Portland Mountain Rescue (PMR),
Central Washington Mountain Rescue (CWMR) and
all the dedicated men and women who volunteer their
time and talents to mountain rescue units.

Special thanks to Michael Leming, John Frieh,
Mark Westman, Paul Soboleski, Lyneen Norton,
Iain Morris, Steve Rollins, Keith Langenwalter,
Hugh O'Reilly, Debra Ross, cascadeclimbers.com
and Virginia Kantra. Any mistakes and/or
discrepancies are entirely the author's fault.

PROLOGUE

JAKE PORTER double-checked the gear in his pack, his motions driven by habit and a sharp sense of purpose. Bivy sack. Avalanche transceiver. Probe. Shovel.

His friends were somewhere up on Mount Hood in the middle of one of the worst weather systems to ever hit the Cascades in December. And Jake was going after them.

Carabiners rattled as he closed the pack. Now came the hard part—waiting.

The other members of the mountain rescue unit sat at cafeteria tables inside the Wy'East day lodge, their faces tight and their voices low as they checked their own gear. Yawning reporters grabbed quick interviews between sips of coffee. Eager photographers snapped pictures of the early-morning mission preparations.

The overhead lights made everything look

pale, stark and ominous, matching Jake's mood. The weather, too.

Outside, visibility sucked. The wind howled at forty miles per hour. The morning temperature hovered around thirteen degrees. The threat of frostbite and the very real avalanche danger made going to a higher elevation a fool's errand. But in his five years as a member of Oregon Mountain Search and Rescue, Jake had never been more eager to confront the elements for a mission.

He wasn't the only one. Every single OMSAR member had responded to the alert. More than a few had already heard the news and been waiting for the call. Others hadn't waited and had come here on their own. All they needed was the go-ahead to start moving out. Up.

Radios crackled as someone asked for additional gear from the rescue cache.

Jake tightened the strap around his shovel, ignoring the knot of concern in his stomach. The whiz of the rough nylon brushing through the buckle intensified his unease. His friends should have made it off the hill with no problem.

Where the hell were they?

Iain Garfield was one of the most talented climbers in the Pacific Northwest. Only twenty-three, he'd already made a name for himself, gaining sponsors and gracing climbing magazine covers with his numerous first ascents of peaks around the world. He could climb the Reid Headwall solo. Backwards. With his eyes closed.

And Nick Bishop. He knew the mountain better than almost anyone in the unit. When they were students together, Nick had once climbed the route overnight and made it to class the next morning for a midterm. After getting married and becoming a dad, he wasn't such a daredevil now. Nick knew challenging the mountain was always a stupid idea. The mountain never lost. That was why after seeing a nasty weather system moving in, he and Iain had changed their plans from a more challenging route to an easier climb.

Radios sprung to life once again as someone asked for the ETA on a Sno-Cat. About time. Except what Jake really wanted was to see his friends walk through the doors with an epic tale to tell.

He stared at the door. No sign of Nick or Iain. Only two rescue leaders talking in hushed tones.

Damn. A heavy weight pressed down on Jake.

Nick had been his best friend since kindergarten class. They'd grown up together. Learned to climb together. Joined OMSAR together. Done everything together. Well, almost everything.

Jake swallowed around the lump of guilt in his throat. He should have been on the climb with them—a climb to celebrate Iain's upcoming marriage to Nick's younger sister, Carly—but Jake had said no. Attending the wedding was enough for him. A climb would have been salt to the wound. Okay, his heart. He thought he'd been following his gut, but maybe the decision not to climb had been selfish. If he'd said yes…

Sean Hughes, one of the rescue leaders who'd been talking by the door, motioned for Jake and two other experienced members, Bill Paulson and Tim Moreno, to come over. "Here's the plan. Avalanche hazard is high and the weather isn't the greatest. A Sno-Cat will take us to the top of Palmer. When we get there, SAR base is expecting us to call in a condition report to decide if we're staying put or if any searching is possible."

Every one of Jake's muscles tensed. At the top of the Palmer ski lift was a building where they could warm up, regroup and wait for the conditions to improve. Sitting around wasn't going to get the job done. They needed to head out in the field.

He zipped his parka. "Nick wouldn't hang around and wait if one of us was up there."

"We're not waiting, either." Sean lowered his voice so no one could hear him. "We'll call in a report, then head up and bring them home."

Jake picked up his pack and swung it onto his shoulders. "Damn straight we will."

The two others grunted their agreement, even though rescuer safety came first in any mission. But when one of your own went missing, risk level changed.

"Let's hit it," Sean said, turning on his headlamp.

Jake followed Sean out of the lodge and into the frigid air. Tim and Bill brought up the rear. The media followed, taking pictures of them, the flashes like lightning, as they trudged their way through the heavy wind and darkness to the Sno-Cat. Freezing mist created a haze on Jake's goggles. Each breath stung. It had to be hell at the summit. What could have happened up there?

Maybe Nick or Iain had gotten injured. Hurt. Maybe they couldn't get cell coverage. Or the batteries had died. Maybe they were waiting out the weather in a snow cave. Maybe—

"Jacob."

The familiar feminine voice wrapped around him like an electric blanket set on high. Soft, warm, perfect. He reminded himself that Carly Bishop's heart belonged to Iain.

But that didn't mean Jake couldn't look and appreciate.

Even with her long, blond hair tucked inside a green ski cap, her cheeks flushed from the freezing temperatures and her eyes red and swollen from crying, she was the best thing he'd seen this morning.

"Carly." He noticed a photographer watching them. The press would sell their firstborn to get an exclusive interview with the fiancée and sister of the missing climbers. "Get inside. It's too cold out here."

She shoved her gloved hands in the pockets of her orange down jacket, which was actually one of Iain's. Her breath hung on the air. "Colder up on the mountain."

Where Iain and Nick were. His eyes met hers in unspoken understanding.

Jake blinked against the biting mist, against the sting in his eyes. "We're heading up to find them."

She inhaled sharply. "Th-they said the search was on hold until conditions improved."

"The conditions are good enough for us."

"Thank you so much." Her eyes glistened with tears. "You have no idea what this means to our family and me."

Jake knew. He was closer to the Bishops than his own parents. That was one reason he'd tried to never treat Carly as anything other than his best friend's kid sister. Well, that, and the age difference. She was twenty-two, four years younger than him. That difference in age meant nothing now, but the gap had been huge when they were teenagers.

Though right now she looked more like a kid than ever. Young and vulnerable. Jake wanted to say something to comfort her, but he hadn't a clue where to start.

"I know it's rough up there and what you're up against. But please, Jacob, do what-ever…everything you can." Carly's voice cracked. "T-tomorrow is…"

December twenty-fourth. Christmas Eve. Her and Iain's wedding day.

Jake had the wedding invitation on his fridge and their gift under his Christmas tree. Tears streamed unchecked down her face. His already-aching heart constricted.

"I promise you, Carly." He wiped the tears off her cheeks with his gloved hand. He didn't dare allow himself to do more, and his caution had nothing to do with the photographer watching them. "I'll find Nick and Iain. Today."

Or Jake wasn't coming back down.

CHAPTER ONE

As SNOW FLURRIES fell from the gray sky, Carly Bishop stared at the charming log house surrounded by towering fir trees and decorated with strands of white icicle lights. A lopsided four-foot-tall snowman, complete with carrot nose, stood in the front yard. A single electric candle shone through a wood-paned window, the flickering flame-shaped bulb a welcoming light.

Carly walked along the snow-dusted path, dragging her wheeled suitcase behind her. A few feet from the porch she noticed a green wreath tied with a red velvet bow hanging from a brass holder on the front door. The scent of pine was sharp in the air. The same way it had been…

Her breath caught in her throat.

The house, the wreath, the candle, the snowman. It was as if time had stopped, as if the last six years had simply been a bad dream.

Any second, Carly expected Nick to fling open the front door wearing a Santa hat, and greet her with a jolly ho-ho-ho. And Iain…

Iain.

She closed her eyes, fighting an onslaught of unwelcome memories.

I can't believe you're going climbing two days before our wedding. Why don't you just admit it, Iain? You love climbing more than you love me.

She'd wanted to forget. The argument and tears before and as he'd left to climb. The thoughts about his selfish behavior while he'd been climbing and dying. The grief and guilt after his body and Nick's had been found.

Carly thought she had forgotten. Put the past behind her. Moved on. She forced herself to breathe.

Coming back had been a mistake.

She should have stayed in Philadelphia, where she'd made a new life for herself, far away from the shadow of Mount Hood and all the mountain had stolen from her. If only staying away had been an option, but her brother's widow, Hannah, was expecting a new baby and needed help with her two children.

So here Carly was. Ready to be an aunt extraordinaire for her niece and nephew. For better or, most likely, worse.

Two weeks. All she had to do was survive the next two weeks, including December twenty-fourth, the twenty-fifth and New Year's Eve. How hard could that be? Given she hadn't celebrated the holidays in years, she didn't want to know the answer.

Carly tightened her grip on the suitcase handle and climbed the steps to the front porch. With a tentative hand, she reached for the doorknob then remembered this was no longer her brother's house. She pressed the doorbell and waited.

The doorknob jiggled.

Straightening, Carly forced a smile. Years of working with customers had taught her how to put on a happy face no matter how she felt inside.

The door cracked open.

"Welcome back, Carly," a male voice greeted her warmly.

She expected to see Hannah's husband of two years, Garrett Willingham, but the man standing in the doorway looked nothing like the clean-cut, non-risk-taking, business-suit-wearing certified public accountant. This guy was too rugged, too fit, too…familiar.

"Jacob Porter." Over six feet tall with brown hair that fell past his collar, he still had piercing blue eyes, a killer smile and a hot, hard body that had made the girls, herself included, swoon back in high school. But those things had only been made better with age. Her pulse kicked up a notch. "What are you doing here?"

"Waiting for you." His grin widened, the same way it had whenever he and Nick teased her about something. "Merry Christmas."

"Merry…" Simply thinking the word left a bitter taste in her mouth. She couldn't bring herself to say it. "Seasons greetings. Where's Hannah?"

"At a doctor's appointment," Jacob explained. "Garrett drove her. She didn't know if they'd be home before you arrived or the school bus dropped Kendall and Austin off so they asked me to come over."

Carly noticed Jacob's clothes—a light blue button-down oxford shirt, khaki pants and brown leather shoes. A bit more stylish than the T-shirts, jeans or shorts and sneakers she remembered him wearing. He must have been at work.

"Thank you." Though she wasn't surprised. Jacob had always gone out of his way for them, a surrogate everything to what remained of the Bishop family. He'd found her the job in Philadelphia. He'd taught Nick's two kids to ski and fish. He'd even introduced Hannah to Garrett.

"Hurry inside before you get too cold." Jacob reached for Carly's suitcase. His hand—big, calloused and warm—brushed hers. The accidental contact startled her, and she jerked her hand away. "You city girls aren't used to the temperatures up here."

Forget the cold. She wasn't used to her response to his touch. Carly couldn't remember the last time a man had had that effect on her. "It gets cold in Philadelphia, too."

As she stepped into the house, heat surrounded her, cocooning her with the inviting comforts of home. She glanced around, noticing all the nice homey touches. Ones missing from her apartment.

"You look the same," he said.

He looked better. She glanced around. "So does this place."

And that somehow made everything…worse.

A fire blazed and crackled in the fireplace. The way it had that horrible, dark Christmas morning when a teary-eyed Hannah had told the kids to unwrap their gifts from Santa.

Carly wanted to close her eyes, to shut off the video of years gone by streaming through her mind, but the fresh evergreen scent, the twinkling multicolored lights and the ornament-laden branches wouldn't let her.

The popcorn-and-cranberry-strung garland, keepsake decorations marking special occasions, and silver bells and gold balls all reminded Carly of the rush to take the tree down before Nick's funeral. Hoping to protect the children, Hannah hadn't wanted the event to be associated with Christmas in any way. Her efforts seemed to have worked, but Carly couldn't think of one without the other.

The door closed. The sound made her glance back.

Jacob stared at her, an unrecognizable emotion in his eyes.

She remembered the time, during an argument with Iain, she'd turned to Jacob for advice. There'd been a moment when she thought he might kiss her. He'd been looking at her then the same way as now.

Her temperature rose—the combo of forced-air heating and fireplace, no doubt—and she shrugged off her jacket.

"I'll take that." He hung her coat on the rack by the door. "It's good to see you again."

"You, too." And she meant that. Funny, but seeing him hadn't brought back any bad memories. That surprised her. "How are things at the Wy'East Brewing Company?"

"Good."

Jacob's family owned and operated a micro-brewery and pub in the alpine-inspired touristy Hood Hamlet, a small town set high on Mount Hood, fueled year-round by outdoor enthusiasts. Nick had worked there. Iain and Carly, too.

That seemed like another life. Who was she kidding? It had been another life.

"Hannah told me things are going well in Philadelphia," Jacob said.

"They are. Didn't you get my last e-mail?" Carly tried to keep in touch with him. Not daily, but an e-mail or two a month.

"I did. She mentioned you had a boyfriend."

"Wishful thinking on her part." It wasn't as if Carly hadn't had any boyfriends over the last six years—okay, two—but both relationships had petered out. "I date, but I'm too busy with work for a serious relationship right now."

"You've really moved your way up the ladder, Miss Brewpub Manager extraordinaire."

"I have, haven't I?" She loved managing the restaurant portion of Conquest Brewery, but Carly had never wanted to be one of those focused career types working megahours. She'd wanted to be a wife. Iain's wife. Boy, had she been young, starry-eyed and idealistic back then. "But I still owe you for getting me that waitress job."

"You don't owe me anything—" Jacob winked "—but if I need an extra hand at the brewpub over the holidays, I'll give you a call."

"Deal." Jacob might be even better-looking than before, but he was still the same inside. She found that…comforting, as well as the memories now surfacing. A smile tugged on her lips. "Do you remember when we would brainstorm names for your seasonal brews?"

"I remember." He shook his head. "Especially the time you wanted to name everything after Macbeth."

Carly grinned. "Hamlet."

"Whatever."

She nudged his arm with her elbow. "Hey, some of the names were quite clever, and considering your brewery *is* located in a hamlet—"

"Yeah, like the guys buying the beer have a clue what a hamlet is."

"Maybe not the exact definition of a hamlet, I'll give you that. But the words 'brewed and bottled in Hood Hamlet' are printed on every single bottle."

Jacob raised a brow. "Nothing could justify naming a seasonal ale, and I quote, 'To Beer or Not to Beer.'"

"That was a great name." She searched her

memory for the others. "Don't forget Lady Doth Protest Porter, Mind's Eye Amber, Less than Kind IPA, Soul of Wit Pale Ale. Instant classics. I'm telling you."

"You can tell me all you want, but that doesn't mean I'll ever use them."

She drew her brows together. "Maybe I should give those names to the master brewer where I work."

"Go for it, but that brewery isn't located in a hamlet so you might have a hard sell on your hands."

"Not if he recognizes genius at work."

"More like plagiarizing at work."

Carly laughed. Jacob's teasing filled an empty space inside her she'd forgotten existed. She had friends—good friends—in Philadelphia, but none who had watched her grow up. Who knew the people who'd mattered most in her life. Who knew what she had been like before being thrown the ultimate curve-ball.

"So what brilliant name did you come up with for this year's seasonal brew?" she asked.

Jacob's eyes met hers. Softened. "Nick's Winter Ale."

The name hung in the air as if a cartoon dialogue bubble surrounded the three words.

Carly swallowed around the snowball lump of emotion lodged in her throat. "The beer he came up with right before…?"

Her life had been divided into two parts—before and after the accident. Things had gotten better with the passage of time. She no longer felt the familiar sting each time she thought about Nick. That dreaded prickling sensation hadn't brought a rush of unexpected tears in…years.

Jacob nodded once. "It's a good brew. He worked hard on it. Seemed time to use the recipe."

Nick had been so proud of the beer he'd created. He had been sure the brew would be the next year's seasonal ale. It probably would have been. "That's wonderful. Nick would be happy."

"That's what Hannah said. Your mom and dad, too."

Carly's parents had divorced after Nick's death. Her father now lived in Oregon. Her mother lived in Scottsdale, Arizona. Both had remarried. "You've spoken to them?"

"Yes, they sounded pleased," he answered. "Each asked for labels and a bottle."

She wasn't surprised. Nick had been the golden boy. No one, not Carly, their grandkids or each other, could fill the gap left in her parents' hearts with his death.

"So do I get any?" Carly asked.

"I have a whole case for you. Labels, too. I'll drop them off."

"Thanks."

"Come on—" Jacob motioned for her to follow "—the kids will be home soon. I need to fix them a snack."

"Wait a minute. You're going to fix them a snack?" The top of her head came to his chin. She looked up at him. "You guys always made me heat up the frozen pizzas and fix whatever else you wanted to eat."

"Good practice for when you're on your own," he said.

"I'll have you know, I've been on my own for—" Six years. She swallowed a sigh.

Jacob didn't appear to notice. "I meant with the kids. They'll expect you to fix their snack for them. And when Hannah goes into the hospital to have the baby—"

"I can handle it." Once upon a time, Carly had dreamed of having children of her own. But like her other dreams, that one seemed to have died on the mountain, too. So she made the most of whatever time she could get with her niece and nephew, meeting them wherever they spent their summer vacation. Anywhere except here in the Pacific Northwest. She hadn't wanted to come back. "Spending time with Kendall and Austin will be great."

His smile crinkled the corners of his eyes, and her heart bumped. "We'll see how you feel in a few days."

Forget a few days. Carly didn't like how she felt right now. But that had nothing to do with her niece and nephew and everything to do with the man standing in front of her. Still, she was a survivor, and like everything else, she would get through this. She raised her chin. "It'll be no problem at all."

No problem. Yeah, right.

Jake had a big problem. Her name started with *C* and ended with *Y*. He grabbed a Granny Smith apple from the fruit bowl and placed it on the wood cutting board.

Maybe if he concentrated on fixing the kids' snack he could forget how Carly's turtleneck sweater hugged her breasts and the curve of her waist. How her well-worn jeans cupped her bottom like a second skin. How her blond hair, now shoulder length, would look spread out over a pillowcase or a man's chest.

His chest.

It was all Jake could do not to stare. Hell, drool. He reached for a knife.

Damn, she looked good. Better than he remembered.

The cold temperatures outside brought a natural color to her cheeks. Thick lashes, ones she'd had since she was little, framed expressive hazel eyes, eyes that no longer held the optimistic promise of tomorrow, but hinted at new depths he hadn't seen before. And those pink, full lips smiling up at him made him think about kisses. And the one time he should have kissed her, but had hesitated and lost her. Not that he needed kisses now. A taste of those glossed lips, simply a nibble, was all he really wanted, but that wouldn't be a smart move.

Hell, it would be downright stupid.

As he sliced the apple, the knife hit the cutting board with a thud.

"Be careful." Carly neatly placed cheese and crackers on a plate. "You don't want to lose a finger."

Right now, he was more worried about losing his heart. Dammit.

His heart was off-limits, especially to a woman who was the only person aside from his father to call him Jacob and had left town six years ago never to return until now. Okay, not exactly true. She hadn't been gone six years. Five years, seven months and twenty-eight days, if he wanted to be exact. Not that he'd been counting.

Granted she'd had her reasons. Good reasons.

But that hadn't made her leaving any easier. Which reminded him. She wasn't here to stay. Hannah had said two weeks. Long enough to turn everyone's life upside-down, including his. He wanted no part of it. No part of her.

Besides, she deserved better than him.

Jake cut another piece of apple.

"The cheese and crackers are ready." She placed an artfully designed plate on the table. "What next?"

"Hot chocolate." He handed her the kettle from the top of the stove.

She frowned. "Won't the water be too hot?"

"If it is, we add ice cubes."

"You've got this kid snack routine down."

Jake put the apple slices and a small container of caramel sauce on a plate. "I help out when needed."

She filled the kettle with water. "How often is that?"

Not nearly enough. He set the plate on the table. "Whenever Hannah or Garrett can't be here."

"They're lucky to have you."

Jake was the lucky one.

A door slammed shut. Thuds of varying volumes echoed through the house. Voices sounded, yelled, screeched.

He glanced at the clock on the microwave. "The bus was early today."

"So a herd of elk hasn't just walked into the house?"

"Elk would be quieter."

With a smile, Carly hurried out of the kitchen. Jake followed her, trying to ignore the sway of her hips. Maybe he needed to go out tonight. Between work and OMSAR activities, he hadn't been dating much. A woman—make that a woman other than Carly—would get his mind right where it needed to be.

"Aunt Carly!" Seven-year-old Austin ran into her arms before she took three steps into the living room. "You're here."

"I told you she was here." Kendall, nine years old, hugged Carly. "I saw a different car in the driveway."

Carly held both of the kids tight as if she didn't want to let go of them. "I can't believe how much you've grown since last summer."

Austin beamed. His blond hair stuck up all over the place. "We're big now."

Carly laughed. "So big."

"Mom asked us to stop growing," Austin said. "But I told her that was impossible."

Kendall rolled her eyes. "Mom was kidding."

"Kidding or not, I understand why she said that." Carly kissed the tops of the kids' heads, staring at them with longing and love. "I wish you would stay little forever."

Watching the three together brought a bittersweet feeling to Jake's heart. The kids needed Carly. Not only when Hannah delivered the baby or when they went on vacations, but also on a regular basis, where they could share their lives and days with their father's sister. With their aunt.

Carly stared at Austin. "You look so much like your daddy."

A perplexed look crossed the young boy's face. "Which daddy? The dead one or the one who's alive?"

Kendall's long sigh could have propelled all the windmills in eastern Oregon. She tucked a blond curl behind her ear. "Our first daddy, right, Aunt Carly?"

"That's right." Her voice cracked slightly.

Jake fought the urge to reach out to Carly. He knew that kick to the gut the first time he'd heard the kids call Garrett "daddy" all too well. Jake still wasn't used to it. He didn't know if he would ever be, even though he liked the guy enough to introduce him to his best friend's widow.

"Every time I see you, Austin, you look more and more like him," Carly continued. "The two of you could be twins."

"Even if they look the same—" Kendall tilted her chin "—Uncle Jake says I'm the one who's more like him."

"It's true," Jake said. Austin might look like a mini version of Nick, but Kendall had identical mannerisms and her father's fearlessness. "You have the exact same personality."

Which made it harder for Hannah and Garrett.

But easier for Jake.

"I noticed that when we were vacationing in Gettysburg," Carly said.

Kendall grinned. "You have to see my room, Aunt Carly. It's purple and blue and green. Uncle Jake bought me this cool, furry beanbag chair."

Carly glanced his way. "Sounds comfy."

"I have a space room." Austin held on to her hand and bounced. "Uncle Jake put glow-in-the-dark stars and planets on the ceiling. He also bought me a spaceship light. It's the coolest."

"Sounds like Uncle Jacob's been busy around here."

He shrugged.

"You mean Uncle Jake, don't you?" Kendall asked.

"Um, yes, your Uncle J-Jake," Carly said, as if testing the name for the first time.

That was the first time he remembered her calling him Jake. He liked how his name sounded coming from her lips.

"I can't wait to see both your rooms." She sounded every bit the enthusiastic aunt, much to the kids' delight. "But first you need to have your snack."

"Snack!" The kids stampeded into the kitchen.

Carly glanced at Jake. "Forget elk, those two could give buffalos a run for their money."

"You handled that well."

She shrugged. "Not much else I can do."

"No, there's not, but that doesn't mean it doesn't hurt."

Carly looked down at the hardwood floor. "They're just kids. And life goes on."

"Hannah does her best to keep Nick's memory alive. So do I."

"Thanks. I appreciate that. Nick would, too." Carly noticed a picture of Garrett, Hannah and the two kids sitting on the mantel. "Still, it's weird. I like Garrett. He's a great guy who adores Hannah and loves the kids as if they were his own, but he's so different from Nick."

"Hannah didn't want another Nick," Jake admitted.

Emotion clouded Carly's eyes. "I don't blame her for that."

"Come here." Jake placed an arm around Carly in a half hug. She leaned against him.

So nice.

Having her in his arms brought back a rush of memories. The time he'd found her shivering and whistling for help when she'd gotten lost snowshoeing at the age of fourteen. As he'd hugged her, trying to warm her up, he'd realized she wasn't a little girl anymore. Or the time she'd passed her driver's test and wanted to show off her license. Not to mention her short skirt and skimpy top. She'd given him a quick hug, letting him know she was a young woman, but still off-limits.

This time she was simply Carly Bishop, a beautiful woman. A single woman.

Against his better judgment, Jake brought his other arm around her, embracing her fully. He pulled her closer. Her body pressed against his. Warm, soft, perfect. The scent of grapefruit—her shampoo?—surrounded him.

Oh, man. Standing here with her in his arms

was a dream come true. And even though he'd long since buried those dreams, Jake didn't want to let her go.

He brushed his lips across her forehead, offering what comfort he could.

Someone screeched.

Jake stepped back from Carly to see Austin staring wide-eyed and openmouthed.

Kendall bolted out of the kitchen. "What is going on?"

"Uncle Jake kissed Aunt Carly." Austin's grin lit up his face. "Now they have to get married."

CHAPTER TWO

MARRIED? TO JACOB? No way.

Carly stared at the kids, jumping and giving each other high fives. She needed to gain control fast or this could set the tone for the next two weeks.

She stuck two fingers in her mouth and blew, the way Nick had taught her. The loud, sharp whistle quieted Kendall and Austin.

Thanks, Nick. Once again her brother had saved her.

Too bad she hadn't been able to do the same for him.

The kids stared at her.

"Into the kitchen," she ordered in the same tone Hannah had used last summer in Colorado when a fight over whether to hike or swim erupted. "And sit at the table."

Even Jacob followed her instructions.

Carly hid a smile as he passed. Suddenly he stopped.

"This is all so sudden," Jacob murmured in her ear with an outrageous flutter of his eyelashes. Long, dark lashes, she couldn't help noticing. Ridiculously wasted on a guy. "Why didn't you tell me? I would have brought a ring."

Heat flooded her face. "Shut up. Sit down."

"Yes, ma'am." He took his place at the table with the kids. No one said anything.

"That's better." Carly followed them into the kitchen. She sat between Kendall and Austin, pushing the snacks toward them. "Why do you think we have to get married?"

"If you kiss someone, you have to marry them." Austin picked up an apple slice. "Sammy Ross told us at recess."

"You don't say." Jacob spoke with the utmost sincerity. "Sammy must be one of those guys who know everything."

Nodding, Austin dipped the apple into the caramel sauce. "He's got five older sisters. Three are in high school."

"That explains it." Jacob winked. "Better watch out who I kiss from now on."

Carly glared. Some help he was turning out to be.

Austin's eyebrows drew together. "You can only kiss the person you're going to marry, Uncle Jake. Aunt Carly."

Uh-oh. She straightened. Damage control was needed right away. "Austin—"

"I know you don't have to get married if you kiss someone, but wouldn't it be great if you got married anyway? You wouldn't have to go back to Philadelphia. And I could be your flower girl." Kendall's brown eyes implored her. "Please, oh, please. I've always wanted to be a flower girl."

Carly's chest tightened. She didn't want to hurt Kendall, but letting the nine-year-old think a wedding was in the works would be worse. The wedding march ranked right up there with Christmas carols when it came to music Carly didn't want to hear again. Besides, she didn't want Jacob to think she was interested in marrying him. It was bad enough Carly thought he was still hot after all these years. "No one is getting married, sweetie."

Kendall's face puckered.

Carly squeezed the girl's small hand. "I'm sorry."

The apology didn't keep the tears from welling in the young girl's eyes. Great, Carly had been with the kids for less than fifteen minutes and already made one of them cry. If this was any indication of how the next two weeks were going to go, she should drive back to Portland International Airport and fly home before she really messed things up.

"Come on, guys," Jacob said. "You're getting a new baby brother or sister next week. Your aunt is here for Christmas. That's plenty to celebrate."

With a frown, Austin stared at Jake. "But you kissed her. I saw you. You have to get married. Those are the rules."

"I only kissed your Aunt Carly on her forehead, buddy. That's what friends do." He flashed her another one of those teasing, tempting grins. "Good friends."

Carly caught her breath.

The gesture had been a little too friendly. As Jacob had comforted her in the living room, Carly had felt a security and a sense of belonging she hadn't felt in years. She'd forgotten everything and hadn't wanted the moment to end. Thank goodness for Austin's screech or she might have done something stupid like kiss Jacob herself. Not on the forehead, but on the lips.

What was going on?

She hadn't wanted to kiss anyone in a while.

Nor did she want to feel compelled to kiss anyone, especially someone who lived on the other side of the country. Okay, she'd once been curious about his kiss, but she'd been a girl then. Not a grown-up. Best to keep her distance from him while she was here.

"So if you kiss a girl on the forehead you don't have to marry them, but if you kiss them on the lips, you do?" Austin asked.

Carly bit back a sigh. "Sammy Ross might think you have to marry the person you kiss, but that's not how it really works."

"How does it work?" Kendall asked.

Feeling like a preschool teacher suddenly taking on a sex education class full of randy teenagers, Carly looked at Jacob for help. He tipped his chair back, clearly content to wait for her response. The devil.

"Well." She wasn't sure how to proceed, but catching a red-eye flight back East sure looked tempting. "First you meet someone you like, then you date, then you fall in love and then, once you know you'll get along for a long time, you marry."

Talk about an abbreviated lesson on dating. Maybe she should have told them to ask their mother instead. But Jacob flashed her the thumbs-up sign. She must have done okay to warrant that or he might have simply been trying to make her feel better.

"Where does the kissing come into it?" Kendall asked.

Carly didn't bother looking at Jacob this time. Hearing a nine-year-old ask about kissing would probably paralyze any single guy. "Kissing can happen at any of those steps, but that's something you do when you're older."

"Much older." Jacob told Kendall. Funny, he sounded more like a dad than a bachelor.

The girl's gaze darted between Carly and Jacob. "But you two could still get married. Then I could be a flower girl."

"We can't get married," Carly said. "We're…friends."

"Shouldn't you be friends with the person you marry?" Kendall asked.

The girl was too smart for her own good. Carly needed to be more careful with what she said. "Of course, you should be friends, but Uncle Jake and I are…more like brother and sister."

Though that wasn't really true. She'd never seen him as a brother. Growing up, she'd wanted him to be her boyfriend.

"He's not your brother though. My daddy was your brother." Two lines formed over

Kendall's nose, the same way they used to on Nick, making Carly's chest tighten. "But if you married Jake, he'd really be our uncle, not just someone we call uncle, and I could be a flower girl, Aunt Carly. Jessica Henry has gotten to be a flower girl twice. And I've never even been asked to be one."

Carly knew what growing up and comparing yourself to someone else felt like. She needed to tell her niece something, even if it meant facing the part of her past she'd tried hard to forget. "Did you know a long time ago, when you were only three years old, you were going to be a flower girl?"

"I was?"

She nodded.

"Was I going to wear a pretty dress?" Kendall asked.

"Yes," Carly said. "A very pretty red dress made out of velvet and taffeta with layers of tulle to make the skirt poof out and a wreath of flowers in your hair."

"You looked like a princess wearing it," Jacob added.

Remembering, Carly smiled softly. "You sure did."

"But I never saw any pictures of me dressed like that," Kendall said.

Jacob started to speak, but Carly stopped him. "The wedding never happened."

Kendall tilted her chin. "Why?"

Why? That question still haunted Carly. "The boy…the man I was going to marry, his name was Iain, had an accident when he was climbing with your daddy."

Kendall's mouth formed a small O. "He died with my daddy on the mountain so you couldn't get married."

"Yes." Carly felt Jacob's gaze on her, but she didn't—couldn't—look his way. She didn't want to see sympathy or pity in his eyes. She'd had enough of that those first few months to last a lifetime. That was one of the reasons she'd left Hood Hamlet and headed to Philadelphia. She'd wanted to go some-where—anywhere—where she could make a fresh start.

"Did I know him?" Kendall picked up a cracker. "Iain?"

Carly nodded. "He thought you and Austin were the two coolest kids around and loved you so much."

"Do you miss him?" Kendall asked.

Carly forced herself to breathe. This was fast turning into the trip home to hell. Not that she blamed anyone, but dredging up the past this way wreaked havoc with her emotions. Ones she'd thought were long under control.

"Yes, sometimes I still miss him." She inhaled deeply. All she wanted was five more minutes with Iain. Thirty seconds would do. To say goodbye with love, not frustration and anger as had been the case. "But you know what? Iain is still with me. The same way your daddy will always be with you. In your heart."

"That's what mommy said," Austin said. He'd been so quiet Carly had almost forgotten he was there. "But I don't remember him at all. Not even when I look at his picture."

"That's okay, buddy." Jacob mussed the boy's blond hair. "You were only a year old."

"That's right. You were just a little guy back then." Carly put her arm around Austin's chair. "But I can tell you lots of stories about your dad if you want. You can remember him that way."

Austin smiled. "Uncle Jake and Mommy tell me stories, but I want to hear yours."

"And you will." Carly cleared her throat. "I know some really good ones."

"I remember him. Our daddy." Kendall got a faraway look in her eyes. "Well, his voice. He used to sing to me."

Carly felt a tug on her heart. She could almost hear Nick's voice drifting down from the nursery upstairs. "Your daddy sang to you all the time. You loved the song 'My Favorite Things' from *The Sound of Music*."

"If he stopped singing that song, you would cry," Jacob said.

Austin laughed. "Crybaby, crybaby."

"Be quiet." Kendall frowned. "You're the one who's a big crybaby."

Austin folded his arms over his chest and pouted.

"That's enough, guys," Jacob said.

Austin returned to his snacks, but not Kendall.

"You know, Uncle Jake," she said. "If you started dating Aunt Carly tonight, you could probably get married before she has to go back home, and I could be a flower girl before I went back to school after winter break."

"Uh-huh. Listen, kiddo—" Jacob stopped, obviously unsure how to proceed. He rubbed his chin.

"You go after what you want, don't you, Kendall?" Carly asked.

The girl nodded.

"Your dad did the same thing." Nick never used to give up when he set his mind on something. That's how he'd ended up with Hannah. Carly smiled at the similarity between her brother and his daughter. "Tell you what. If I get married, you can be the flower girl and Austin can be the ring bearer."

"Promise?" The girl's hopes and dreams filled the one-word question.

"Your aunt said *if*, not *when*," Jacob clarified. *If* being the key point, and Carly was grateful for him pointing it out.

"But if you do, Aunt Carly…"

Even Austin leaned toward her in anticipation of her response.

She smiled. "I promise."

Married? To Carly? Too funny.

Jake could barely contain his laughter when the kids had brought that up, but the way she'd sent dagger-worthy glares his way kept him quiet.

Poor Carly. Those kids had pushed every one of her buttons. Some twice. With a shake of his head, he carried Carly's suitcase upstairs.

She followed behind him. "I'd forgotten all about the wall of infamy."

He glanced back and saw Carly staring at the photographs. "You mean wall of family."

She didn't take her eyes off the pictures. "I call it as I see it."

"Me, too."

Eight years ago, he had dreamed about being a real part of the Bishop family, of having his photo up on that wall. A wedding photo. He'd wanted to be Nick's brother-in-law, Carly's husband. And then, while Jake was taking his time waiting for her to grow up, Iain had taken his shot at happiness. The daring young climber had almost blown it though, and given Jake another chance, but when all was said and done, Carly stuck with Iain after he apologized for putting a climb before her birthday.

At the time, Jake told himself everything worked out for the best. But it hadn't.

Not for Iain, killed right before his wedding.

Not for Carly, widowed before she was a bride.

Not for Nick, dead before his time.

And not for Jake, either.

He continued up the stairs.

But what had happened or how he had felt about Carly was in the past. All that remained was for him to make sure she was happy and living life the way she should. Once he knew that, then he, too, could move on.

"Hannah will run out of wall space someday." He glanced back and saw Carly still staring at the pictures. "Or photos."

"Wall space perhaps," she said. "But thanks to digital photography, Hannah will never run out of pictures."

"True, she carries her camera everywhere."
He listened to the kids in the kitchen doing
homework. "Hope that wasn't too much for
you downstairs."

"Well, it's not every day you get into a head-
on collision with your past."

"Good thing you had an air bag to soften the
blow."

"What air bag?" Carly asked.

"Me."

"Oh, yes, that thumbs-up was a huge help."

"You were doing great on your own." He re-
spected the way she handled the situation. "I
just provided a little cushion."

Her mouth twisted on one side. "How can
Mr. Hard Body be a cushion?"

He grinned, remembering the teasing from
years gone by. "I'll take that as a compliment."

"You would."

Jake laughed. "Still the pesky little sister
shadowing her big brother, aren't you?"

"Being here brings it all back." The amusement had disappeared from her voice. "But
that's not such a bad thing. Living so far away,
it's easy to forget."

He entered the guest room and placed the
suitcase on the bed. "Everyone's missed you."

"I've missed them."

Jake had missed her, too. But he saw a new maturity in her, a difference from the girl she'd once been. That hadn't come across in her e-mails. He liked the changes.

"The promise you made to the kids," he reminded. "They will hold you to it."

"I expect them to."

"So you plan to marry someday."

She shrugged. "I've learned you can't really plan on something like that. But if I met someone and fell in love…well, maybe I'd want to marry him."

Not the answer Jake was looking for. "You don't sound like the girl who started reading bridal magazines when she was sixteen."

"I haven't met anyone I've wanted to marry…."

Except Iain.

Though Jake wondered how marriage to an adventurous, full-time climber would have been for Carly. Still, the fact she hadn't seemed to have gotten over Iain's death made Jake feel guilty. Okay, guiltier.

"But you could." He wouldn't be happy until she moved on with her life the way Hannah had. Carly deserved a happy ending, too. Jake would somehow make sure she found one. He owed her that much.

"I could." Carly didn't sound that confident as she opened her suitcase.

Jake didn't blame her. He hadn't known what to make of Iain the first time he'd met him. The kid's confidence bordered on cockiness, but Jake had soon learned the talented climber had a heart of gold. He couldn't help but like and respect Iain. Envy him, too. For his fearlessness. For his climbing talent. For being the recipient of Carly's love and adoration.

At least until finding Iain's bloody, bruised and broken body covered in snow. The image had given Jake nightmares for years. He blinked, hoping to erase the picture in his mind. "You really should."

Another shrug. "Do we need to check on the kids?"

He listened to the sound of voices drifting upward. "Nope. I hear them."

"I thought it was good when kids were quiet."

"Noise is good," Jake said. "Quiet means start worrying, but I can hear them. We'll help them with their homework later."

"What about you?" Carly asked.

"My homework days are long past."

"That's not what I'm talking about." She picked up a black camisole from her suitcase and threw it at him. The same way she'd tossed a dishrag or a sweatshirt at him years ago.

He caught it as he always had. "Nice throw."

But the action felt too intimate to Jake in a way it never felt before. This was the kind of top a man peeled off a woman.

Pink tinged her cheeks. "Sorry, habit."

"It's okay." Jake handed her the top rather than tossing it back to her. "What did you want to know?"

"Have you given marriage much thought?" she asked.

He was hoping she wouldn't go there, but maybe after coming home to face her demons—and the devil kids downstairs—she deserved the truth. It wasn't as if the information would change anything between them. "I was engaged, but other than that…"

Her gaze met his. "Nobody told me. You never told me."

He shrugged. "It was four…no, five years ago."

"So what happened?"

His jaw tensed. "I don't want to talk about it. I barely remember it."

He'd wanted to forget. While Hannah and Carly had been holding themselves together, he'd been falling apart.

"Come on. Tell me," she urged. "Did you kiss her and then have to get married?"

If only it had been that simple.

"Not exactly." Jake wasn't proud of what he'd become or done back then. "I was partying too much, met a woman who was nice but totally wrong for me and asked her to marry me. Luckily I realized getting married wasn't the thing to do at that time in my life so I broke it off."

And got his out-of-control life back together.

"Do you ever think about settling down now?" Carly asked.

"No. I see no good reason to change the status quo."

She grinned. "That's what I say, too."

Jake found her words hard to believe, even harder to take. Her joy and excitement over her upcoming wedding to Iain seemed a hundred and eighty degrees away from where she was coming from now, and that hurt. She was meant to be a bride.

Someone else's bride, Jake reminded himself.

He didn't deserve her.

If he'd been on the mountain six years ago with Iain and Nick, everything would have been…different. Better. Okay.

And it was up to Jake to make things right.
For Hannah, Kendall, Austin and…
Carly.

CHAPTER THREE

PATRONS PACKED the bar and dining area of the Wy'East Brewing Company. Carly hadn't seen so many familiar faces since…

She felt a pang in her heart.

Since Nick's and Iain's funerals.

With a sigh, Carly glanced around the lodge-style building. Jacob's place. She could see the care he'd taken with it, the improvements he'd made to the interior and the menu offerings since taking over after his father retired.

The aromas of beer and grease mingling and wafting in the air reminded her of the brewpub she managed back home. The conversations of customers drowned out the music being piped in through speakers. At least Christmas carols weren't playing.

Too bad everything else was decked out for the holiday.

A swag decorated with miniature lights, pine

cones and holly berries hung around the bar. Wreaths dangled from the vaulted log-beamed ceiling. A twinkling Christmas tree sat in the corner next to a small stage with neatly wrapped packages underneath.

Talk about being dropped in the middle of a nightmare before Christmas…. She shifted in her seat. Since arriving in Portland earlier today, she'd been forced to confront the worst moments of her life over and over again.

"Your adoring crowd awaits," a glowing and very pregnant Hannah teased.

Carly forced a smile. She didn't want to leave the comfort of this table, but she couldn't hide behind her sister-in-law's family for the next two weeks. Hannah was obviously excited. And Carly wanted her sister-in-law to be happy.

Fortified by a serving of shepherd's pie and a salad topped with raspberry vinaigrette, she stood. Working her way through the jam-packed restaurant, she received hugs while having the same conversation over and over again.

Yes, she lived in Philadelphia now.

No, she wasn't married yet.

Yes, it had been a long time.

She missed Iain, too.

Carly could hardly breathe as she spoke. Facing her demons was one thing, but this… She plodded through the way she had six years ago at her brother's funeral and then at Iain's, gritting her teeth and smiling. This time, however, the answers got easier to say the fifth time around. They became automatic by the tenth. Progress? Carly hoped so.

She looked around the room once more. She'd expected to see Jacob at some point this evening. This was his brewing company. His pub. Where was he on such a crowded Wednesday night? She brushed aside a twinge of disappointment.

It wasn't easy to do. If Jacob were here, he would make this not such an ordeal. He would make her feel normal, the way he had at the house, and comfortable.

After what seemed like hours but was really only one, Carly reached the spot where she'd begun. The dinner plates had been cleared from the knotty pine table. A pitcher of beer had joined the kids' and Hannah's pitcher of root beer. A slice of half-eaten mud pie and five spoons sat between Hannah and Garrett.

They were sharing. Happy.

There was no reason for Carly to be here.

And no one for her to be with.

She swallowed the pint-size lump in her throat and sat opposite them. "Hey, you love-birds. Where are the kids?"

"With Jake," Hannah said.

So he was here after all. "I didn't notice him."

"He's been here the entire time."

And he hadn't come over to say hello? At least, not until she left the table.

Ouch.

Carly rested her elbows on the table and supported her chin with her hands. Making the rounds down memory lane had drained her mentally and physically. The last thing she needed to worry about was Jacob Porter.

"Sorry that took so long," she said. "I can't believe all the people I know who are here tonight. Most of the local OMSAR members, too."

"Word's out you're back in town." Garrett looked at Hannah. "Though I can't imagine who would have told them already."

"I may have mentioned it to a few people," said a sheepish Hannah.

"That's a good one, my beautiful wife." Garrett laughed. "Since your definition of a few ranges from two to two hundred."

"I'm sorry," Hannah said.

Carly bit back a sigh. She didn't want Hannah to feel bad. Besides, if Carly got all the hard stuff over with her first day in town, she could breeze through the rest of the trip. "Don't apologize. Now I won't have to search people out since I saw them all here tonight."

Hannah tucked her shiny, long, auburn hair behind her ears. "That's the spirit."

"She's being a good sport, my dear." With a smile, Garrett poured a pint from the pitcher containing a deep, amber-colored beer. He slid the glass in front of Carly. "Here. You earned this."

"Thanks." She appreciated Garrett's thoughtfulness, as well as the way he honored Hannah's past, making sure Nick's memory stayed alive with the kids and accepting Carly as a part of their family. "I really need this."

"Yes, you do." Hannah's green eyes danced. "It's Nick's Winter Ale."

Carly should have known. A jumble of emotions ran through, but the biggest one—pride—made her raise her glass. "To Nick."

"Hear, hear." Garrett joined in the toast. "To the brewmaster extraordinaire."

"And Iain," Hannah added.

Carly took a sip. She wanted to remain impartial, to judge the beer on its own merits, to…

Delicious. Refreshing. Absolutely perfect.

The velvety smooth ale struck a perfect balance between the malt and hops. Full-bodied with a hint of cinnamon. She had never tasted something so yummy. Of course, Carly wouldn't have expected any less from her big brother.

"Extraordinaire is right." Her smile couldn't begin to match the joy in her heart at Nick's accomplishment. "An awarding-winning winter ale if I ever tasted one."

Two hands rested on her shoulders. Large hands. Male hands.

Jacob.

No need to turn around and see he was the one standing behind her. She'd recognize the warmth of his touch and his familiar scent anywhere, even in a crammed brewpub with all the noise, sights and smells competing for attention.

He gave a gentle squeeze, but didn't move his hands away.

The gesture, no doubt meant to be platonic, sent unexpected tingles shooting out from the point of contact. Carly gulped. She hadn't experienced tingles in…years.

No big deal.

"From your lips to the judges' scores," Jacob said.

She glanced up at him. "It's delicious."

His gaze met hers. "I'm happy you like it."

"My new favorite."

"Mine, too. Especially if it keeps that big smile on your face."

The way he stared at her, as if she were the only woman in the room, made Carly's insides clench. Her temperature shot up. She looked away.

"Thanks for putting the beer into production." She watched a bead of moisture run down her glass. "It means…a lot."

"I know."

Carly got the feeling he knew a little too much. She took another swig of her beer, but the liquid did nothing to cool her off or help her relax.

So what if he still had his hands on her shoulders?

No big deal.

He might still be a total hottie, but she wasn't a schoolgirl with a crush on her brother's best friend. No reason to freak out.

Jacob removed his hands. Thank goodness. Carly blew out a puff of air.

As he sat on the bench next to her, his thigh brushed hers. More tingles and a burst of heat erupted where he'd touched her. She scooted away. "Where are the kids?"

"In my office playing cards," he said. "They finished their ice cream sundaes and were still hungry so I gave them cookies."

Hannah tsked. "You spoil them, Jake."

"I indulge them," he countered. "A big difference."

His easy grin made him look younger and so carefree. Compared to him, Carly felt old and troubled.

Sure, she was home for the first time in years surrounded by family and old friends. Laughter and cheers filled the air, a good time being had by all the smiling faces. But something was missing.

Not something, Carly realized.

Nick and Iain.

She looked across the table at Hannah, resting her head on Garrett's shoulder. How did she handle this? Not just evenings like this, but every night, every day, raising Nick's kids in his house, in his hometown where memories lay waiting around every corner.

Somehow Hannah had found the hope and the courage to love again. And had made her peace with the past.

Not Carly.

She had barely made it through dinner tonight.

She stared at her bare hands. There hadn't been an engagement ring on her finger for years—never a wedding band like Hannah had worn. And yet…

Carly glanced sideways at Jacob, her cheeks warming. She almost felt guilty for being so aware of the man sitting next to her. It seemed strange to be feeling this way, for reacting to his nearness and his touch. This was where Iain had tended bar and she waited tables. Where they would have celebrated their rehearsal dinner had he made it down the mountain.

But he hadn't made it down. And she hadn't died up there with him even though it had felt like that at the time.

Losing him and Nick had hurt so bad.

She had wanted only to forget, but perhaps it was time to follow Hannah's example and remember.

Instead of avoiding the past, Carly could try to embrace it. Maybe then she could finally put the pieces of her heart back together and learn to love…again.

Chasing a woman was never a good idea.

It ranked right up there with "Don't talk back to your father" and "Don't glissade down a mountain wearing crampons."

The next day, Jake's feet crunched through the ice-crusted snow covering the sidewalk.

"Carly," he yelled.

No response.

He could see her bright purple jacket as she paused outside Wickett's Pharmacy.

That was what had caught his eye. The purple jacket.

Jake had been standing by his office window—talking back to his dad, actually—when she hurried by on the sidewalk and he saw her cell phone drop from her pocket.

Returning it seemed like a good idea. A good deed. It sure beat arguing with the formidable Van Porter over his desire to review the brewery's most recent financial statement.

Except now Jake was chasing after Carly Bishop.

Running, not chasing.

"Carly," he called again.

She stopped and turned. "Jacob?"

He caught up to her. "Why do you keep calling me that?"

"Because Nick once told me you didn't like it."

"And here I was being a nice guy and returning this to you." He waved the slim, red rectangular gadget in the air. "Maybe I'll keep it."

"My phone?" She reached for it, but he raised the phone over his head. "No fair."

"Who said anything about playing fair. Finders keepers—"

She made a jump for the phone, but missed.

"Nice try."

Carly pursed her lips. "In case you forgot, *Jacob,* you and Nick used to tease me unmercifully and order me around like I was your maid or something. Calling you by your full name was my small way of getting back at you."

"What did you do to Nick?" Jake asked.

"I turned all his underwear pink."

"That wasn't very nice."

"The two of you following me on my first date with Iain and sitting behind us at the movies heckling wasn't nice, either."

He laughed, remembering. Nick hadn't trusted any guy with Carly. "We may have been a little rough on you."

"A little?"

"Okay a lot." He placed the phone on the palm of her gloved hand. "I found this on the sidewalk outside the pizza parlor."

"Thanks. I had no idea I dropped it. Must be my lucky day."

His, too.

Carly looked great in her parka, jeans and boots, the way she had at the brewpub. When she had stared up at him with those warm, clear hazel eyes of hers and smiled, he felt as if he'd fallen into a deep crevasse. Climbing out hadn't even entered his mind.

"Thanks, too, for dropping off the beer and the labels." Carly tucked the phone into her pocket, but this time she zipped it closed. "The kids were sorry they missed you."

Kids, not her. Not that Jake expected her to miss him.

"Did you have fun sledding?" he asked.

"A lot of fun. Though Kendall and Austin like to go so fast. I was sure I'd have to break out the Band-Aids."

An SUV drove past and honked. Mr. Freeman, who owned the general store. Jake and Carly both waved.

"You used to go pretty fast yourself," Jake said.

Carly grinned. "I was faster than you and Nick."

"We let you think that."

Her mouth gaped as a group of snowboarders walked around them. "You did not."

"We didn't," he admitted. "But we told ourselves we did."

Her smile returned.

Good, he thought. She needed to smile more.

A comfortable silence settled between them, but the rhythm and sounds of the hamlet continued.

Down the sidewalk, Muffy Stevens knocked icicles off the awning in front of the coffeehouse. A truck driver delivered boxes of produce to the corner café. Laughing skiers entered a local inn.

"No matter how some things change," Carly said finally, "other things stay the same. Same locals. Even the tourists."

"And my dad."

Sympathy filled her eyes. "Still having trouble with him?"

"Like you said, some things don't change." Jake glanced across the street at the brewpub. "He's been retired for two years, but still wants to control things at the brewery. He doesn't think I have it in me to take the business to the next level."

Now why the hell had he told her that?

Jake rocked back on his heels.

"It's got to be hard for him to let go," she said. "To move on."

"Yeah, must be."

Blond hair stuck out from her wool ski hat.

Jake fought the urge to push the strands back under. He stuck his hands in his pockets instead.

Was it time to move on?

Or time—finally—to make his move?

Carly glanced at the town hall's clock tower. "I'd better get back to Hannah and Garrett's."

"Okay."

But it wasn't. Not really. Jake didn't want to say goodbye.

"I'll let you go, then." For now, he thought. "But let's grab dinner sometime."

Her pretty mouth dropped open. "But—"

"Friday," he said, as if she hadn't spoken. "Hannah doesn't go into the hospital until next week. I'll pick you up."

"I—"

"Seven o'clock tomorrow night," he continued, before she could say no, and left without looking over his shoulder.

Move on.

She needed this. And so did he.

At two-thirty in the morning, Carly sat at the kitchen table with a steaming cup of herbal tea. Snow fell outside the window. The snowplows would be working overtime to keep the roads clear.

She took a sip of the chamomile tea. The box claimed the blend would make the drinker sleepy. She sure hoped so. She hadn't had a good night's sleep since arriving in Hood Hamlet.

Carly wanted to blame her sleeplessness on the three-hour time difference between the East and West coasts, but she knew that wasn't the reason behind her restless nights. Every time she turned around the past seemed to collide into the present, from being here with Hannah and her family to walking the streets of Hood Hamlet to reach the post office. Not to mention Jacob...make that Jake...

She hesitated to call their upcoming dinner a date. The word *date* made her nervous. Besides, he hadn't given her a chance to say yes or no. She didn't know what to make of that.

Or...him.

Footsteps sounded in the hallway. Hannah waddled into the kitchen, wearing a turquoise fleece robe that didn't cover her pregnant belly. "I thought I heard someone get up."

"Sorry if I woke you."

"Trust me—" Hannah patted her tummy "—I wasn't sleeping. This little jelly bean started kicking as soon as I lay down and hasn't stopped."

"Want a cup of tea?" Carly asked.

"No, thanks." Hannah lowered herself into a chair. "If I drink anything, I'll be going to the bathroom every five minutes instead of every fifteen. I keep reminding myself I wanted to get pregnant again."

"The end result will be worth it," Carly said.

"I know, but I have to admit, I'm happy they're taking this one early. I don't want to be birthing a ten-pound baby. Austin was hard enough at nine pounds six ounces."

She grimaced.

"Don't worry," Hannah said. "They make babies cute so you forget what you go through during labor and delivery."

Carly laughed. "So what's on today's agenda?"

"I want to finish up the last batch of Christmas cards, get them in the mail and do some shopping if the roads are clear. I wanted to be finished with all the holiday stuff by now, but it hasn't happened."

Carly did her holiday shopping in September before any of the red and green decorations hit the stores and carols played nonstop. She wasn't particularly organized, but Christmas had become so entwined with the accident she wanted no part of it. "I can take your cards to the post office."

If she dropped them into the box outside, she could avoid any more reminders of the holly-jolly season.

"That would be great. But I'm out of Christmas stamps. Would you mind—?"

She drew a deep breath. "No problem." So, she'd have to actually go into the post office. It wasn't as if Hannah had asked her to brave the mall with the kids or do any of those other things she avoided doing in December. All Carly had to do was buy stamps. "I'll take care of it."

"Thanks." The only light in the kitchen was from the stove, but Hannah's smile lit up her face. "That will be a big help. I don't have the energy to stand in line. Not to mention I'm as big as a mail truck."

"No, you're not." Carly wrapped her cold fingers around her warm cup. "Just tell me what needs to be done. That's why I'm here."

"How is being back here going for you?" Hannah asked.

Carly took another sip of tea, the warm liquid coating her dry throat. "Fine."

"Fine as in everything's great or fine as in not really, but I don't want to bother you?"

"Something in the middle of those two."

Hannah rubbed her lower back. "Want to talk about it?"

"Not really."

"That bad, huh?"

"Not bad, it's just being back here has been a little…strange." Carly stared into her cup of herbal tea. "I look around and I can't help but wonder…"

"What?" Hannah asked.

This had been the elephant in the room Carly had avoided talking about. This probably wasn't the right time, either, but with the kids around she never had Hannah to herself. And Carly really needed to talk about this. Now more than ever.

"It's just…" She took a deep breath. "If I had convinced Iain not to climb instead of fighting with him, Nick wouldn't have died."

The only sound in the kitchen was an occasional ice cube dropping into the bucket in the freezer.

"Nick made his own decision to climb that day. He could have said no," Hannah said finally.

"I should have told Nick not to go." Carly stared at her fingernails. "Iain was upset when he left. If he was distracted… If his mind wasn't in the right space—"

"Accidents happen. It wasn't your fault. It wasn't anyone's fault."

Carly wanted to believe that. Desperately. "I still wish I would have talked Iain into staying home."

"And I wish I had told Nick to stay home," Hannah admitted. "But we can't change what happened. All we can do is live our lives the way Nick and Iain would have wanted us to live."

Carly reached across the table and squeezed Hannah's hand. "That's what you're doing. Nick would be so proud of you. I admire you so much."

Another ice cube clattered into the plastic bin.

"I climbed it," Hannah said, her voice a mere whisper in the dead of night.

It. The mountain. Carly shivered. "When?"

"Three years ago. In May. Jake and Sean Hughes took me up." Hannah stared out the window. "I wanted to stand on the summit the way Nick had done so many times and see what he saw. So I could try to understand."

"Understand?"

"Why he loved climbing so much." Hannah sighed. "I used to consider the mountain my nemesis. Mount Hood. The other woman in our marriage."

Carly understood completely. Iain had his eye on peaks around the world, including Antarctica. "I sometimes wondered who Iain loved more. Me or his mountains. Who he would have chosen if he could have picked only one of us."

"He loved you. Just like Nick loved me and the kids." Hannah tilted her chin. "But the mountains held an allure for them. Nick thrived on the mental and physical challenges of climbing, but he told me once the mountains were the place he found joy and felt most comfortable."

"Were you comfortable up there?" Carly asked.

"No, I was scared to death," Hannah admitted. "I didn't know if I could make it to the top. I remember standing in the parking lot at Timberline and looking up, thinking it was so far away. And it was. The slog up to Palmer took forever. The sulfur smell from the Devil's Kitchen made me so nauseous I thought I might throw up. I wanted to stop, but when I saw the triangular shadow of the mountain to the west Nick had told me about so many times…I had to keep going as much for myself as him. It wasn't easy. The ice on the Pearly Gates intimidated me, but I knew I was so close."

Carly listened, totally amazed by what Hannah, who had a paralyzing fear of heights and had never climbed anything in her life other than stairs, was telling her.

"Standing on the summit was…surreal." Hannah sighed. "All that snow and ice. I was so tired, completely wiped out by the climb, and I felt so small compared to everything around me, but there was such a sense of accomplishment. Of having made it to the top of something so big when I didn't think I could.

"The views were incredible and took my breath away. Jake had pointed out where Nick would have crossed the saddle of Illumination Rock to get to the Reid Headwall. It didn't matter that I couldn't see where the accident happened. I just thought about Nick and how he'd stood here and seen the same things. The morning sun glimmering on the Columbia River. The line of snow-capped volcanic peaks running to the north and south. All these other beautiful sights below me. I felt so…so close to him, as if he were right there with me, and everything was okay again. I could finally understand and not hate what he loved doing or this mountain where he'd died."

"Wow."

"It was definitely wow worthy, but I have no desire to climb again. I couldn't wait to get back down." The corners of Hannah's mouth turned up in a satisfied smile. "But I got the closure I wanted. Needed. And that's what you need to do yourself."

Carly's heart slammed against her chest. "Climb Mount Hood?"

"You've already done that."

Not since Iain had taken her up and proposed on the summit.

"You need to find whatever it is that will give you closure so you can move on," Hannah continued.

"I have moved on."

Hannah raised her eyebrows.

"Really," Carly insisted. "This trip has been good for that."

"And Jake?" Hannah asked. "Where does he fit into all this?"

A beat passed.

"We're friends."

Hannah drew her brows together. "Are you sure that's all you are?"

The concern in Hannah's voice and eyes sounded an alert in Carly's head. She straightened. "What do you mean?"

"Well, you liked him when you were younger."

Had her feelings been so transparent to everyone? Carly sighed. "Jake was my brother's best friend and always around. It was safe. A crush, nothing else."

"But he has asked you out to dinner."

"It's not a date. At least, I don't think it's a date."

"Uh-huh." Hannah used the table to help her stand. She rubbed her lower back again. "And what does Jake think?"

CHAPTER FOUR

MOVE ON? Or make his move?

Jake wasn't sure what he wanted as he sat across from Carly at Mama Amici's, a family-run Italian café. Things were not going well. The din of conversations from other customers only intensified the silence between them. He never expected tonight to be so damn uncomfortable.

Forget about what he might want. He needed to think about what Carly needed. Doing that, Jake knew exactly what he needed to do—re-connect with her as a friend. One who'd watched her grow up and cared about what happened to her. His job was to make her smile, laugh and relax so when she returned to Philadelphia she would be ready to move on. To love again.

Love someone else.

Jake shifted in the booth. Might as well jump on it. "It's just you and me here, Carly. No need to be nervous."

She placed the napkin she'd been toying with on her lap. "Do I seem nervous?"

So far, she had spilled her water, dumped the contents of her purse and dropped her knife onto the floor.

Jake shrugged. "Maybe a little tense."

"It's been a while since I've been…"

"Out to dinner," he offered.

She tilted her chin. "I had dinner at your brewpub the other night."

"That's right, and you didn't look as tense there." He swirled his glass of Chianti. "Or keep eying the door like you're ready to bolt."

"Sorry." Carly glanced around the restaurant until her gaze rested on the flickering votive candle on their table. "It's just…this feels sort of like a date and I'm not sure what it's supposed to be."

"It's not a date. Dinner with a friend."

He'd purposely picked this casual mom-and-pop café with its vinyl-covered booths and red-checked tablecloths so the evening wouldn't feel like a date. He hadn't wanted her to get the wrong idea. Hell, he hadn't wanted to get the wrong idea himself.

"If this was a date," Jake continued. "I would have taken you to a place where the smell of garlic doesn't smack you in the face when you walk in the door. You know, one of those fancy places where the waiter shakes out your napkin for you and they make you sniff the cork."

The corners of her mouth turned up. Her lips opened, giving him a clear view of her straight, white teeth. Those braces she'd complained about for three years had been worth it.

But he still wanted to see a full smile, one that reached all the way to her eyes. Time to send it.

"And I would have brought you flowers," he added.

A wide smile erupted on her face. Score.

"You bring flowers?" She stared up at him through thick lashes, and Jake felt as if he'd been kicked in the gut. "Roses or daisies?"

"Different kinds of flowers," he said once he could breathe again. "Roses or daisies or whatever was your favorite."

"Sounds lovely."

She was lovely.

"I'd only bring those if this was a date." Which this wasn't, he reminded himself. "But I would never think of asking you out on a date."

Liar. Jake swirled the wine in his glass. He should have kept his mouth shut.

"Never? Once I thought… Well, it doesn't matter."

Damn, she was onto him. Suddenly bolting out of the restaurant didn't seem like such a bad idea after all. Instead, he met her gaze. "Okay, yeah. But I got over it."

Over you.

"Oh." Carly's mouth quirked. "That's good. Less awkward for everyone."

He smiled ruefully. "It would be hard to beat this for awkwardness."

"Oh, I can beat this."

"Please do, and take me out of my misery."

"That bad, huh?" she teased.

Jake shrugged.

"Okay." Amusement filled her eyes. "After Iain's funeral, someone came up to me to express his condolences. He also offered to be my friend with, um, benefits though his words were a little more blunt and left me speechless."

Jake's temper flared like lightning. "Who was it?"

"No one you knew," she said.

"Carly."

She sighed. "It was one of Iain's climbing friends from up north, a guy not worth the effort or a police record. Otherwise I would have asked you to beat him up."

"I still could have pushed him around a little."

She grinned. "Oh, one of your steely glares would have definitely intimidated him."

"What did you do?" Jake asked.

"Well, I didn't know whether to laugh it off or slap him. I couldn't stop thinking this was someone who Iain planned to climb with after we returned from our honeymoon. All of a sudden, the tears started flowing and wouldn't stop. The guy shoved his cocktail napkin into my hand and disappeared. I never saw him again."

"A good thing."

"No doubt, but that wasn't nearly as awkward as…"

She ran her fingertip along the stem of her wineglass.

"Tell me," Jake urged.

"Iain's parents." She took a sip of her wine and placed the glass on the table. "They showed up at the apartment the day after the funeral. I know they were in shock like me, but they acted like total strangers. They wanted any items Iain had left there and all the wedding gifts his family had sent. His mother kept picking up things and asking if they belonged to Iain. And then his father told me not to expect anything from Iain's estate since we weren't married. As if that's all I cared about, not the fact my hopes and dreams had died on the mountain with their son."

She didn't sound bitter, simply resigned.

"I had no idea." Jake reached across the table and touched her hand. "You should have told me."

"I didn't tell anyone, not even my parents."

Her skin felt soft beneath his fingers, the way he had imagined it would feel. "Thanks for telling me now."

As a comfortable silence descended, an invisible connection drew them closer. Wanting to reassure her, he squeezed her hand.

She smiled.

He smiled back.

"Out of your misery?" she asked.

"Completely. Thanks." Jake realized his hand still covered hers. He didn't want to move it, but did, lifting his fingers off her smooth skin and reaching for his wineglass. "But you might be the miserable one now."

"I've never been better."

He studied her face. No tightness around her mouth or creases on her forehead. "I believe you."

"You should."

Jake did. "Something's different about you."

She nodded. "I finally realized I can look back, but still move forward. It's been…good."

Those were the words Jake wanted to hear, but he wanted to make sure she didn't stop. "Keep at it. Those dreams of yours can still come true."

"I hope so."

"I know so."

"Thanks." Carly raised her glass. "To old friends."

"Hey, we're not over the hill yet."

"You're older than me."

"Only by four years."

"Well, you made it seem like a lot more when we were younger." She kept her glass raised. "Always taunting me about being older and wiser."

"I was older and wiser," Jake said. "And you could be a real pest."

"Oh, so me being a pest justified you comparing me to poison oak?"

She still made him itch.

He cleared his throat. "Admit it. You used to follow us everywhere. Spying. Annoying us."

"That's what little sisters do."

But she wasn't little any longer. And she sure wasn't his sister. "I wouldn't know. I'm an only child. But it looks like you've outgrown the pest stage."

"You sure about that?" she asked.

Her gaze, full of laughter and warmth, held his. Uh-oh. He felt as if he were treading where he shouldn't, traversing below a slab of snow ready to release and carry him off a cliff into the abyss below. He couldn't allow that to happen.

To old friends.

Jake tapped his glass against hers. The chime hung in the air. "Cheers, my friend."

As Jake drove his SUV along Highway 26, Carly pressed her head against the passenger seat's headrest. She couldn't believe how much fun she'd had with him. She wasn't looking forward to saying goodbye. "Thanks for dinner tonight."

"I hope we can do it again," Jake said.

"Me, too."

She meant the words. Being with him was so easy. Once they got through the initial silence and determined this evening wasn't a date, they could talk and joke. She couldn't remember the last time she'd felt so close to or so at ease with anyone.

And that worried her.

Carly liked keeping her distance, even with the few guys she'd dated, but surprisingly things had gotten downright cozy between her and Jake at the cute little Italian café. Oh, strictly platonic in spite of his holding her hand once. But another dinner for two, even a friendly meal, probably wasn't a good idea.

"Next time we should include Kendall and Austin," Carly added.

"The more the merrier," Jake replied easily.

His ready acceptance of the kids bothered Carly. She loved her niece and nephew, but a part of her wished he could have sounded a little disappointed at not being alone with her again.

Pathetic.

She glanced his way. The lights on the dashboard glowed, silhouetting his strong jaw and his straight nose. So handsome. Gorgeous really. If you liked that type. Which she did. Unfortunately.

Just friends.

She forced herself to look away.

The headlights illuminated a swath of snow-covered trees. The temperature outside had to be below freezing, but she felt a little toasty. Must be the hot air from the heater.

Yeah, right.

And maybe she'd wake up in a couple of days and discover Santa had left her the perfect present under the tree. She sneaked another peek Jake's way.

Too good-looking for her own good.

Better watch it.

He turned into the driveway, shifted the gear stick into Park and turned off the engine. He opened his door, hopped out and walked toward the front of the car.

Panic struck. She didn't mind the little man-woman gestures that added spark to a relationship. But she didn't want them from Jake. A two-week fling with an old friend who shared so much history with her wasn't a good idea.

Carly opened the door and slid out of the SUV. Her feet landed with a thud and sunk through the layer of new snow. She lurched toward the porch. Her foot slid on the layer of ice beneath the powder.

Oh, no. She slipped and tried to balance herself.

"Whoa." Two hands wrapped around her and held her upright. "It's icy out here. You need to go slow or you'll fall."

She felt as if she'd already fallen. No way could she get up without help.

His warmth and strength enveloped her. Her heart pounded. She struggled to breathe. She looked back at him. "Th-thanks."

A slow grin spread over his face. "At your service."

Heaven help her. She wanted his… No, she didn't.

Carly shivered and crossed her arms over her chest.

"It's cold out here." He removed his hands from her. "Let's get you inside."

Yes, because a list of words describing their dinner was running through her mind. Comfortable, cozy… If she weren't careful the next word on the list would be *couple*.

Not that Jake would want to be part of a couple with her. Or bring her flowers. Or kiss her good-night.

Kiss her? She really needed to say goodbye and get away from him.

Carly hurried toward the front steps, careful so she wouldn't slip again. Jake followed. She stood at the front door, her hand gripping on the doorknob, feeling tongue-tied and all twisted up inside.

"Good night, Carly." He lightly tapped the end of her nose. A platonic, totally unromantic gesture.

She shouldn't complain. That was what she'd wanted from him. Not a date. No kisses required.

"'Night." She moistened her dry lips. "Thanks again. For everything. I had a great time. I really did."

She needed to stop talking. Now.

"You should come with us tomorrow," Jake said.

"Us?"

"I'm taking the kids to their ski lessons. Kendall and Austin love to show off what they're learning."

The kids. Not just Jake. Carly could do that. She appreciated the invitation. Besides, knowing Jake, he would be off skiing himself.

"Thanks, I'd love to go." She remembered her Saturday lessons when she'd been a kid. "I haven't been to Ski Bowl in years."

Jake hesitated. "The lessons aren't at Ski Bowl."

Her heart dropped. "Timberline?"

He nodded, his eyes serious.

"I can't go."

"I understand, Carly." Compassion filled his voice. "But remember what you said at dinner. About looking back, but still moving forward."

"This is different." She took a deep breath. "You're not asking me to look back. You want me to stand in the one place where my dreams began and ended."

"Maybe this is something you need to do."

Carly couldn't go back there. "Maybe it's not."

"There's only one way to find out."

She stared at her feet. "I don't know."

Jake raised her chin with his fingertip. "I do."

Carly couldn't believe she was standing at the edge of one of Timberline's freestyle terrains with an old pair of snowshoes strapped to her feet. Snow flurries fell from the gray sky, but the temperature didn't seem that cold. What gave her the shivers was the summit behind her. If not for the kids, she could have never done this. The kids and...well, Jake.

He stood next to her and gave a thumbs-up sign to Kendall.

Carly readied her camera to catch the next run. She concentrated on the kids and picture taking. Anything to keep her attention focused down the hill.

The top of Mount Hood held too many memories, both good and bad. Dealing with the bright Christmas decorations, the sparking lights on trees and the overflowing holiday cheer inside the Wy'East day lounge had been difficult enough when they'd dropped the kids off for their ski lesson. Carly couldn't handle seeing the summit this close up, too.

Jake adjusted his sunglasses. "We can grab skis and hit the slopes ourselves."

And get even closer to the top. No way. "Thanks, but I'll stick to snowshoes. You go ski."

"I'd rather stay here with you."

She was grateful for his understanding how hard being here was for her, but a part of her—the same one as last night—wished he would leave her alone. Of course, the other part wished he wanted to be with, well, her.

Face it. He'd been on her mind when she'd closed her eyes last night and opened them this morning. She couldn't help herself. The guy was a total babe magnet, drawing second and third glances from females of all ages on the slopes, including herself.

Who could blame any woman for checking him out? In his red soft shell, black pants and a red patterned ski cap, he looked as if he'd taken a break from a photo shoot or stepped off the page of a ski magazine.

A good thing his sunglasses hid his eyes. Toss in those pretty baby blues and he'd be pretty darn irresistible.

To the other women, that was.

Not her.

Kendall, dressed in black bibs and a polka-dotted blue parka, waved at them. With a big smile on her face, she lowered her goggles from the top of her sticker-covered pink helmet.

"Is this how you spend every Saturday?" Carly snapped a picture. "Watching the kids in ski school?"

"Nope. Garrett usually brings them, but with the baby coming I thought he and Hannah could use some alone time."

Carly stared at Jake in amazement. "You're too good to be true."

A wry grin formed on his face. "I know a few women who would disagree with that statement."

"Only a few?"

He laughed. "The kids have really progressed with their skiing."

"Don't change the subject," Carly said, curious about the women in Jake's life. "We're friends. Friends share things, right?"

He shrugged.

"Come on."

"There's not much to say except most of the women I date are looking for more than a Saturday night date."

"What do they want?"

"A wedding date. A wedding date of their own," he clarified. "Since marriage isn't something I'm interested in, they aren't too happy when I won't get serious with them."

"Serious?"

"Make a commitment."

"So have you caught up to Sean Hughes with the number of hearts you've broken?" Carly teased.

"Nope, Sean still holds that record. I'm not even close to him."

"Not yet anyway."

"Though I may be able to catch up a little now that Sean's heart has been spoken for."

"Who's the lucky lady?" she asked. "A gorgeous snowboard model?"

"Close," Jake said. "A beautiful Siberian husky named Denali."

"I can't believe Mr. I-don't-let-anything-tie-me-down has a dog."

"Believe it." Jake pointed to the kids. "Kendall's turn."

As her niece sped toward a ramp, Carly held her breath and raised her digital camera. No wonder Hannah didn't like watching the kids ski. Whether they were skiing down a run or doing jumps, it was nerve-racking.

Kendall flew into the air, executed a twist and landed solidly as Carly took a picture.

Carly exhaled and clapped. "She is so much like Nick."

"Told ya," Jake said.

"You did, but Kendall reminds me of someone else, too."

"Who is that?"

"You," she said. "I know the kids have a step-father now, but you have done an amazing job with them."

"Thanks. That means a lot to me."

"You mean a lot to Kendall and Austin. They talk about you all the time."

"Maybe now, but they're young. Soon they'll be teenagers and won't be so keen on spending time with their Uncle Jake."

"I doubt that."

"They are growing up so fast."

"I know." Carly watched Kendall talk to her instructor. "Remember when you and Nick took Kendall skiing for the first time?"

Jake smiled. "Hannah wanted to kill us."

"Kendall was only two."

"She did great," he said. "But Hannah wouldn't let me take her back out skiing. I had to wait until she started kindergarten. Austin, too."

Austin skied down another run with his class. The kid liked to go straight and fast. No fancy jumps or unnecessary turns for him. She aimed the camera at him. "Doesn't seem to have hurt her. Or Austin."

"Guess not." Jake's tone was far from indifferent.

"But you wanted them on skis," she said.

He focused on Austin, who had stopped to wait for the rest of the class. "It's what Nick would have wanted."

"And that's why you've gone above and beyond for Hannah and the kids all these years." It wasn't a question because Carly already knew the answer. "You've taught the kids about the outdoors. You introduced Hannah to Garrett. You've made sure what Nick would have wanted for them came true."

Jake shrugged. "I did what any best friend would do. Nick would have done the same for me."

Except Jake didn't have a wife and two kids. He didn't even have a pet. Just a father who never thought he was good enough.

"You're a good friend, Jake Porter."

"Sometimes." He pulled her hat down over her eyes. "Sometimes, not. I haven't been that good a friend to you over the years."

She pushed up her hat so she could see. "I'm the one who left and never came back."

"You had good reason," he said. "But your heart never really left Hood Hamlet. You can take the girl from the mountains, but you can't take the mountain out of the girl."

"I'm not exactly a girl anymore."

"Even eighty-year-old women still have a

girl inside them. And before you ask, my grandmother told me that."

"Grandmas know everything."

"Mine thought so."

The two ski classes continued down their respective runs until the kids disappeared down the hill. Carly shivered, fighting a chill. She raised the collar of her jacket.

"The temperature dropped. Let's grab a hot chocolate in the lodge," Jake said. "The kids still have another hour of ski school."

"Sounds good."

In the bar on the second floor of Timberline Lodge, light streamed through the tall windows. Carly sat on a love seat opposite Jake, her huge mug of cocoa on the coffee table between them. They were the only two customers. "This really hits the spot."

As it always had in the past.

Some things never changed. Timberline Lodge was one of them. The historic building's timber and stone construction had a very northwest feel. The arts-and-crafts decor was comfortable and understated. But her favorite part had always been the view of the mountain from the Ram's Head Bar.

Carly tried not to look, but couldn't help herself. The large windows provided picturesque views of Mount Hood. The summit peeked through the clouds.

"Beautiful," Jake said.

The glimpse of the snow-covered peak where Iain had proposed and died was bitter-sweet.

She'd waited here for Iain and Nick to come down that fateful December day. She wasn't sure where things stood between her and Iain after the fight, and she'd needed to know. So she'd sat, watching the hours tick by until she realized something had to be wrong, terribly wrong, and she'd called the one person who would know what to do—Jake.

"I'm not sure what to think of the mountain even though it's been six years," she admitted.

"Sometimes it still feels as if everything happened yesterday."

"I know." Carly hadn't thought anyone else felt like that. "And the what-ifs…"

"Are still hell."

"They can drive you crazy."

He looked at the mountain. "If I could do it all over again, I would have climbed with them that day."

She shuddered. "You might have been killed, too."

"No, I *know* I would have made a difference

and all three of us would have walked off the mountain together."

How many times had she dreamed that scenario? Too many to count.

"But I thought I was following my gut instinct by not climbing," Jake continued. "Instead I was being…"

"What?"

"Selfish."

The recriminatory tone of his voice clawed at her heart.

"It wasn't your fault." She found herself repeating the same words Hannah had said the other night. "I've never blamed you for not being with them. Hannah hasn't, either. I'm happy, relieved, you name it, that you weren't up there. I don't know how any of us would have made it through without you."

"Thanks for that." He sipped his drink. "What happened was an accident, but knowing that hasn't gotten rid of all the guilt."

Carly knew exactly how he felt. She wanted to help him. "Did you ever consider your gut instinct wasn't wrong? That your decision not to climb wasn't selfish, but self-preservation?"

He stared out the window at the mountain. "I never thought about it that way."

She reached across the table and touched his hand. "Maybe you should."

He nodded.

"Is there anything else that might help you?" she asked.

A beat passed. "You."

Her heart slammed against her chest. She pulled back her hand even though she wanted to still be touching him. "M-me?"

"Nick and Iain would want you to be happy."

"I'm…" Not exactly happy. She wasn't going to lie to Jake. He deserved better than that. "I'm doing okay."

Which was the truth. Not happy, not great, but okay. Nothing wrong with that.

"You've built a life for yourself in Philadelphia, but something seems to be holding you back. Someone. Iain, perhaps."

She stared into her mug.

"Think about what you said about moving forward," Jake said. "It's time for you to get on with your life, Carly. Fall in love, get married and have those kids you always talked about having. That's what Nick and Iain would have wanted for you to do."

"It's not that easy."

"Especially if you won't let anyone get close to you."

"Have you been talking to Hannah?" Carly asked.

"She's worried about you. I am, too."

"I'm trying." She appreciated his concern. "You said you felt guilty about what happened. So do I."

"Why?" Jake asked.

"Because of that terrible fight Iain and I had over the climb. I should have tried harder to make him stay home, then Nick wouldn't have gone."

"Iain would have soloed the route."

"You're probably right." Carly took a breath. Iain lived to climb. Nothing would hold him back. Not even her love. She'd often wondered what marriage to someone like that would have been like over the long term. Probably not as wonderful as she'd thought at age twenty-two. "Okay, you're absolutely right, but Nick wouldn't have been with him. Hannah would still have her husband. Kendall and Austin, their father. You, your best friend. And me…"

"Your brother." Jake rose from the love seat opposite Carly and sat next to her. "Looks like both of us have been thinking along the same lines."

"We probably should have talked about this."

He placed his arm around her. "At least we're talking about it now."

With a nod, she leaned against his shoulder. He felt so warm. Strong. She wanted to soak up his strength. Him. "Hannah told me Nick and Iain made their own choices. No one's at fault."

"She's told me the same thing. Many times."

"Maybe it's time we listened to her."

He nodded.

"Seeing Hannah and Garrett together as a couple and so in love has made me realize there are second chances," Carly said. "Want to know what's helped the most?"

"What?" Jake asked.

"Actually a who. You."

He stared at her for what seemed like forever.

She didn't know if what she'd said was wrong, but it's how she felt. He was caring and understanding. Gorgeous and sexy. He had made a difference, and she wanted him to make even more of a difference in her life. Somehow. She moistened her lips. "I'm sorry, I shouldn't have—"

A wide smile broke across his face. "Yes, you should have."

She looked up at him with anticipation. She opened her mouth to speak, but he never gave her a chance to say a word.

His lips covered hers with such tenderness.

He kissed her as if this was the beginning and the end. As if he was afraid to ask for too much, but unable to keep himself from taking more.

She had never felt so special, so cherished, than in this moment.

His kisses heated her from the top of her head to the tip of her toes. Better than rich hot chocolate. Smoother than the dollop of whip cream floating in her mug.

His lips moved over hers gently.

Her heart felt as if it were finally waking up after a restless sleep. Her blood heated and surged through her veins. Desire, long forgotten, made her lean toward him.

Carly loved how his kisses made her feel. She didn't want the kiss to end.

But slowly he drew back from her. She stared up at him. The longing in his eyes brought tears to hers.

Jake brushed a strand of hair away from her face. "That was better than I imagined it would be."

Her heart skipped. "You imagined kissing me?"

He stared at her as if she was the last woman on earth. "Once or twice."

Her throat clogged with emotion. She remembered that one time. "When?"

"A while ago."

"Before…"

He nodded. "A long time ago."

Carly had been right. He had thought about kissing her. But she wasn't sure how knowing that made her feel. Flattered. Desired.

Unsettled.

She stared out the window, at the mountain as the backdrop to all the most memorable events of her life, and all she could see, all she could think about, was Jake. The past, the present, the future.

His kiss had totally rocked her world.

Carly couldn't remember Iain's kiss ever having such an affect on her. She must have forgotten.

Oh, no. How could she forget her fiancé's kiss?

Sure, she'd kissed other men in the past six years, but not one of them had made her forget Iain. She couldn't believe it would be Jacob Porter because that complicated…well, everything.

"Jake…"

"Shh." He placed his finger on her throbbing lips. "It's okay."

But Carly knew better. "No, it's not."

Jake had always been there. For Hannah. For the kids. For Carly.

She'd just gotten him back in her life. Did she want to risk that? For what? A few toe-curling kisses.

"We're friends," she said.

He grinned. "Good friends."

Her treacherous heart skipped another beat. Oh, no. "Hannah and the kids count on you."

"So?"

"With the holidays and the baby…" Her voice trailed off. She looked at him, willing him to understand. "I count on you."

"I'm glad."

He didn't get it at all. She tried again. "But what happened…"

"You mean my kissing you."

As her cheeks warmed, she nodded. "Kissing changes things. Complicates things. I like to keep things simple."

Simple equaled safe.

"What are you getting at?" Jake asked.

"I like you, Jake. A lot. But maybe it would be better if we stayed just friends. Friends who don't kiss," she added in case he still didn't get it.

From the look on his face, he did.

CHAPTER FIVE

LYING IN BED, Jake heard a ringing in his ears. Bells? He opened his tired eyes. The noise stopped.

Maybe he was imagining things. He felt completely wiped out. Carly's kiss had burned, branding itself on his lips, his brain and his heart. One kiss shouldn't have had such an effect on him. Yet thoughts about it and her had kept him awake past midnight.

Friends who don't kiss.

She'd given him a taste of heaven only to send him straight into "just friends" purgatory. He wanted to change her mind, but the worry in her eyes and the tightness around her lovely mouth had kept him from saying or doing anything. She'd been out of his life for so long. He didn't want to blow it by not listening to her. A temporary, strategic retreat was in order, but he wasn't about to roll over and play dead. He would think of a way to change her mind. More kisses were definitely in order.

The ringing sounded again.

Not bells. The telephone.

Adrenaline surged. Jake knew what a call at this hour meant. Someone was in trouble somewhere. OMSAR's alert system sent out pages, phone calls and e-mails when the sheriff called for assistance.

Sometimes the calls came during the day. Many times they came in the middle of the night. Each situation was different.

Reaching across the bed for the phone, Jake glanced at the digital clock on the nightstand. 3:23 a.m.

Next to the clock, his pager lay silent. That was odd. The alert system was automated. Usually he got paged for a mission, too.

He picked up the receiver and hit the talk button. "Porter."

"Hey, Jake. Hannah's water broke," Garrett said matter-of-factly. "The doctor wants her to go to the hospital now."

Jake jumped out of bed. He knew what "now" meant when it came to delivering babies. At least Hannah's babies. He headed to his closet. "She's not supposed to be induced until after Christmas."

"That was the plan, but it looks like we're going to need to hang another stocking on the fireplace." Garrett sounded calm, a little tired, but nothing to suggest something out of the ordinary was going on. Of course, the guy never lost his cool or got riled up. That was one reason he'd been the perfect addition to OMSAR's board of directors. Garrett Willingham could always be counted on to be the voice of reason. "Think you can pick one up for us?"

"No problem." Jake didn't understand the lack of urgency in Garrett's voice. "Did the doctor say go 'now'?"

"As soon as we can. Luckily, Hannah hasn't started contractions yet. Getting to Portland in this weather might take a while."

Jake glanced out the window. White flakes falling from the sky limited his vision. Uh-oh. Not good. He brushed his hand through his hair, a little concerned.

"I'll call everyone." One big, happy family sounded like a cliché, but the handful of OMSAR members who lived on Mount Hood year-round helped each other out. Even those who didn't live nearby were willing to lend a hand, too. Good times, bad times. At the beginning of a new life or at the end of another. "We'll get you there."

"That's what I told Hannah. She still needs to pack, but is doing laundry instead. Her way of keeping control of the situation."

"Forget control," Jake said. "Remind her how fast Austin came."

"She told me you almost had to deliver him."

"Yep, and I never want to have to go through anything like that again." Jake might be a wilderness first responder and have EMT training, but the last place he wanted to stick his head and hands was between his late best friend's wife's legs, even if it was to deliver her baby. "I doubt she does, either."

"That may get her moving faster," Garrett said. "Thanks."

"Get her packed no matter what she says or wants to do. I'll be there ASAP."

And that meant Jake would see Carly. Good. He hadn't liked the way she'd bolted out of his SUV like a downhill skier on a run for Olympic gold when he'd dropped her and the kids off. Usually women didn't want him to leave, not the other way around.

He made the calls as he dressed, then climbed in his SUV. The weather combined with the snow on the road made the driving tricky, even with four-wheel drive and studded tires. Headlights came toward him. He recognized the large pickup truck with a snowplow attached to the front and waved.

Sean Hughes leaned out his window and his Siberian husky, Denali, stuck her head out, too. "What took you so long, Porter? Did you stop for an espresso first or did you need to put your date back in its pen before you took off?"

Jake ignored him. Sean always had something to say, anything from a smart-assed comment or a joke to diffuse the tension when they were out in the field. He also had no problem speaking his mind, which made him a favorite with the local media. But underneath that gruff exterior was a guy who would go out of his way for anyone, friend or stranger.

"How's the road looking?" Jake asked.

"Clear to the house. I'm heading to the highway now." With a nod, Sean rolled up his window and drove off.

Jake continued on to Hannah and Garrett's house. The plowed road made for easier driving. Jake parked and jumped out of his truck. The cold wind blasted him, and the snow pelted his face.

Floodlights illuminated the driveway where two OMSAR members—Tim and Bill, who Jake had also called—blew snow away. White icicle lights added a festive glow to the house.

Granted, this wasn't the first time an OMSAR member made a middle-of-the-night hospital run to deliver a baby in a snowstorm, but if they didn't hit the road soon, this was going to turn into a damn birthday party.

Inside the house, the combination of the furnace, fireplace and bodies wrapped him with warmth, chasing away the early-morning chill. He hung his jacket and hat on the rack by the door. A bunch of familiar OMSAR faces, including paramedic Leanne Thomas, greeted him. Obviously, more calls had been made after his.

"The gang's all here," Jake said.

Leanne winked. "Gotta take care of the money man."

Garrett had been elected OMSAR's treasurer two years ago. He didn't ski or climb, but he knew finances and had become a valued behind-the-scenes unit member.

"Not to mention the money man's wife."

Nick's widow.

The words went unspoken.

The smell of freshly brewing coffee and the sound of all the conversations going on brought back images from six years ago. Almost to the day, in fact. But the mood was one hundred and eighty degrees different. This was a celebration of life. New life.

Jake glanced around. The twinkling tree lights, the Christmas cards hooked with clothespins on rope and interspersed with the kids' artwork made Jake think about family and home. Thanks to the Bishops, he'd always had those things.

"Garrett's trying to get things together for the hospital, but he could really use help," Leanne said. "Use some of that infamous Jake Porter charm and convince Hannah it's time to finish packing?"

"Where is she?"

"In the kitchen."

At least Garrett had gotten her out of the laundry room. "On my way."

Hannah sat at the table with a pen in her hand and a piece of paper in front of her. Carly, dressed in jeans and a bulky brown sweater, peered over her shoulder.

The sight of Carly took Jake's breath away. She looked like she needed a good-morning kiss. He could use one himself. Damn, she was sexy. Her tousled hair looked as if she'd crawled out of bed and not even brushed her fingers through it.

Voices drifted in from the living room. Sean Hughes must have been on a cell phone with someone in there because he offered to lead the drive to the hospital. Leanne wanted to ride with Hannah in case she went into active labor and needed help. Other people chimed in to the discussion. Hannah, however, paid no attention to them or to anyone. She seemed to be in no rush to get to the hospital and kept writing.

"That's enough for me to get started, Hannah," Carly said, her tone concerned and her attention focused only on her sister-in-law. "You need to finish packing so you can get to the hospital."

"There's no rush. I'm not showing any signs of labor."

"Your water broke."

"My water broke prematurely." Hannah kept scribbling. "I'm not due for two more weeks. Remember, they were taking this one a week early. Contractions aren't going to start until they induce me so let me finish this list for you. You're going to need it."

The underlying worry of Hannah's words was clear to Jake.

Damn. He rubbed the back of his neck. For once he wanted something to go Hannah's way. She'd been through so much already. The last thing she needed to worry about was having the baby two weeks early and not being ready. But like it or not, she had to get moving.

"Good morning, ladies," he said. "I hear the jelly bean decided not to wait until next year to celebrate Christmas."

"Surprised us all, I must admit," Hannah joked. "Too bad I don't have a My First Christmas bib or outfit to take to the hospital with me."

She looked up at him. Jake expected to see a smile, not a hint of fear in her eyes. He wasn't used to seeing her like this, and he didn't want to say anything to upset her more.

Instead, he poured himself a cup of coffee. "Christmas is still two days away. We'll find a First Christmas outfit complete with Santa hat. Right, Carly?"

"Uh, sure," she said. "We'll find one."

"Come on, Hannah," Garrett said from the doorway. "It's time. I'm going to wake the kids so you can say goodbye."

"I need to finish my list."

"Honey, I know this caught you off guard, but we need to go. You can finish the list later."

Hannah clenched her jaw. "I'm not in labor."

"The doctor said—"

"The doctor is a man and, like you, has no clue about these things in spite of all his credentials and the initials behind his name." She glared at a taken-aback Garrett. "I will go to the hospital when I'm ready to go. Right now I'm busy, so leave me alone. Please."

Garrett started to say something, but Jake raised his hand to stop him. The guy might be Hannah's husband, but Garrett hadn't been through this before with her. Jake had. Twice. Tonight made it a hat trick. He motioned he would take care of it. With a nod, Garrett left to rouse the kids.

As Hannah continued writing, Jake took a sip of coffee. He watched the clock. A minute passed. "All packed and ready to go?"

"Almost. I need to finish this first," Hannah said.

Her stalling tactics bothered him. When she'd gone into labor with Kendall, Hannah had been in a rush to get to the hospital. She'd buzzed around the house like a hummingbird that couldn't find a flower while a pale Nick talked to the doctor, trying to figure out if they should go yet. Jake hadn't known what to do, so he'd helped Hannah get into the pickup truck and wished Nick good luck. Jake had shown up later that day at the hospital with a six-pack for the new dad, flowers for the new mom and a stuffed bear for Kendall.

Those had been the days. So young, so naive, so stupid back then.

With Austin, there hadn't been time to do much except to get in the car and drive with a lead foot. The labor hit hard and fast. Hannah couldn't reach Nick, who'd been climbing, so she'd called Jake. The baby's head was partway out by the time they made it to the hospital. Nick had arrived during the pushing, allowing Jake to get the hell out of there.

He took another sip of coffee and glanced at the clock once more. "Time's up, Hannah. You can finish the list later. Right now, you've got to go."

She dropped her pencil, staring at her list.

"You don't understand." Her voice cracked. "Having this baby early is going to ruin the kids' Christmas. I was hoping to finish everything up today, but now Carly's going to have to take care of it and she needs to know what to do. Otherwise—"

"Carly and I will make sure the kids have the best Christmas ever." He set his coffee on the counter and kneeled at Hannah's side. "Isn't that right, Carly?"

Her eyes met his in understanding. He saw the same worry on her face as he felt. The two of them had to get Hannah moving and on her way. "The most totally wonderful Christmas ever," Carly added.

Tears welled in Hannah's eyes. "But…I promised the kids I'd take them to see Santa today."

"We'll take them," Carly said.

Hannah glanced back at her. "Are you sure?"

Carly nodded. "It'll be fun."

Jake touched the top of Hannah's hand. "Just concentrate on delivering the newest addition to the family. Carly and I have everything else covered. No worries, okay?"

"There's really no rush," Hannah said, her gaze darting between the two of them.

"You know that," Jake said. "But for those of us who have never had a baby, would you please go to the hospital now?"

"I suppose."

"Thanks," he said quickly, not wanting her to change her mind.

"I should be the one thanking you." Hannah hugged him and squeezed Carly's hand. "I'm lucky to have both of you. So are the kids."

As Jake stood, Carly mouthed a thank-you to him. Seeing her lips move reminded him of kissing her. A spark of heat shot through him.

Hmmm. This could be the opportunity he needed, a chance to spend time with Carly, pint-size chaperones aside, and show her how they could be friends and still kiss. Jake grinned.

If things went the way he hoped, this might turn out be his best Christmas ever.

No matter where Carly went, she couldn't escape Christmas.

She stood in the mall surrounded by everything she'd avoided for years and never wanted to experience again. The over-the-top decorations, the teeth-grinding Christmas music and nonstop holiday cheer were driving her crazy.

Today, the sixth anniversary of Iain and Nick's fateful climb, was not the day she wanted to battle Christmas. Unfortunately, Carly had no choice.

Maybe this was the ghost of Christmas past's idea of a joke? She closed her eyes, hoping it would all disappear, but when she opened them everything seemed brighter, louder, sparklier. She tried thinking about something other than the Christmas nightmare surrounding her, but her thoughts shot straight to one thing…make that person—Jake.

His kiss yesterday had opened the physical floodgates. She needed to close them. She didn't want to be led by emotion, by a physical need or desire of anybody.

Carly wasn't ready to go there yet. Especially with Jake, the subject of her childhood crush and teenage fantasies.

For someone who wanted life to be simple, hers had suddenly gotten very complicated. But she couldn't be concerned about herself right now.

She thought about Hannah in a hospital bed, worried and missing precious holiday traditions with her kids. More was at stake than Carly's comfort level. Kendall and Austin's Christmas rested in her hands. Okay, Jake's hands, too. They had promised Hannah the kids would have the best Christmas ever. They would have to work together to make sure it happened.

Together.

Talk about complications.

Carly rubbed one side of her forehead, trying to keep the headache threatening to erupt at bay. She wove her way through the throngs of shoppers, balancing bags and packages, while pushing strollers and holding young children's hands. Her packages were safely hidden in Jake's SUV so the kids wouldn't see them.

"Aunt Carly." Kendall waved. Her green sweater with a kitten wearing a Santa hat was hard to miss. "We're over here."

Here being the North Pole Village, home to the ambassador himself of this holiday horror, good old Kris Kringle. Kendall and Austin stood in a long line of children. Some in pretty party dresses, others wearing simple play clothes. All were accompanied by ragged and tired-looking parents, but where was…

"Where is Jake?" Carly asked, surprised she didn't see him nearby. He knew better than to leave the kids alone.

"He's at that store over there buying us smoothies," Austin said, pointing.

"Don't worry, Uncle Jake sees us or he never would have left us here by ourselves." Kendall sounded so much like Hannah. "He watches us like a hawk."

"That's because your Uncle Jake loves you so much," Carly said.

"Yep." Austin grinned. "He spoils us rotten."

"That's for sure." Carly wouldn't mind being spoiled a little. Not by Jake, but someone. Someday.

She looked around. The jolly fat guy wasn't sitting on the big red throne. No wonder the line hadn't moved. "Where is Santa?"

"He had to feed his reindeer," Austin said.

"And it's taking forever," Kendall complained.

"I'm sure he'll be back." Carly noticed the bag in Kendall's hand. "What did you buy?"

"A stocking and a First Christmas outfit for

the baby." The girl bubbled with excitement. "There's a little red hat and matching bib, too."

"Sounds cute," Carly said, grateful Jake had thought to buy those. That would make Hannah feel better.

Austin moved closer to her. His wide brown eyes stared up at her. "Has Mommy had the baby yet?"

The concern in his voice squeezed Carly's heart. These poor kids. First they lost their dad and now their mom had to say goodbye to them in the middle of the night. At least they had Christmas to look forward to.

Carly placed her arm around his narrow shoulders. "Not yet, honey, but she will have the baby soon and then we can go to the hospital and meet your new baby brother or sister, okay?"

Austin nodded. "I hope it's a boy."

"I just want a healthy baby," Kendall said.

Austin's eyes narrowed. "Sammy Ross says all babies do is spit up and poop. Is that true?"

Carly bit back a laugh. Unlike the kissing and having to get married, this time Sammy was correct. "Well, newborns don't do a lot. They drink, cry, sleep, dirty their diapers and spit up."

"Yuck." Austin crinkled his nose. "Sammy said they smell. I hope our baby doesn't smell bad."

Carly bit back a smile. "You'll love your baby."

"Not if it smells."

She mussed Austin's hair. "Just you wait. The smell won't matter. You're going to be a great big brother."

Just like your daddy was to me, she thought with a pang.

Jake arrived with four smoothies in a drink tray. He handed a cup to each of them. Carly appreciated his thoughtfulness, but then again, as he'd proven buying those things for the baby, he was that kind of guy. Friend, she corrected.

"Thanks." She sipped her pink smoothie through a straw. The cold liquid tasted so good going down her throat. "Raspberry. My favorite."

"I know."

Carly was flattered he remembered after all these years. When she was around Kendall's age, maybe a little older, she'd memorized all of Jake's likes and dislikes. Not that bringing him a frozen Milky Way bar had endeared her to him in the slightest. He hadn't noticed she existed. At least not in the way she'd wanted him to notice her. They'd been like a Western Meadowlark falling in love with a Chinook salmon. Two different creatures. Two different ecosystems. The two weren't meant to be together. She stirred the smoothie with her straw.

"Look, it's Santa." Awe filled Austin's voice. "He must have finished feeding the reindeer."

The delight in the boy's eyes brought a smile to Carly's face. The way the children responded to the holiday was almost magical. She'd forgotten about that.

Santa hobbled past, using a cane as he walked. Not bad. Real beard, wire-rimmed glasses and rosy cheeks. He was better than some of the other Santas she saw when she was a kid.

"Sorry that took so long, children," Santa said. "But Vixen and Dancer wanted seconds."

The kids giggled.

"Do you think he brings his cane with him in his sled?" Austin whispered.

"I don't know," Carly answered honestly.

"You can ask him," Jake said.

Soon the line moved, and before she knew it, they were stepping through a white gate that had silver snowflakes painted on it. As Kendall watched the dancing penguins, mimicking their movements and singing along to their song, Carly videotaped her.

A singing snowman captured Austin's attention. He made Jake explain how everything worked, from the robotic movements to the sound coming from a tree. Jake's patience reminded Carly of her father. Her nephew's curiosity reminded her of Nick.

She pushed aside the bittersweet thought. This needed to be a happy day for the kids. The best Christmas ever was going to be a tall order for her and Jake to fill.

"Do you know what you're going to ask Santa to bring you?" Carly asked.

Both kids nodded.

"I want a snowboard," Austin said. "And a pirate ship."

"I want an iPod," Kendall said. "And makeup. But Santa already knows this because we sent him a list. We're here for the picture today."

Too smart for her own good. Hannah and Garrett had better watch out. "You can still tell him in person."

"Do you know what you're going to ask Santa for, Aunt Carly?" Kendall asked.

"I have everything I need right here." Carly glanced from Kendall to Austin, and then looked over at Jake. He looked so comfortable here, surrounded by this manufactured North Pole and the two kids. The way he casually rested his hand on Austin's shoulder made him seem more like a dad than a family friend who'd been made an honorary uncle. Carly had never imagined Jake Porter as a father before, but now she could see it so clearly. Her mouth went dry. "No need to ask for anything else."

Kendall pouted. "It's Christmas. You have to want something, Aunt Carly."

"Maybe she wants Santa to bring her a boy-friend." Jake emphasized *boy*.

Kendall drew her brows together. "That might be hard for Santa's elves to wrap, Uncle Jake."

Carly struggled not to laugh.

"If you tell Santa what you want," Austin said to her, "you'll get a candy cane."

"A candy cane, huh?" Carly asked. "Maybe I'll have to think of something. Got any ideas?"

"A video game system," Austin suggested. "Or a robot."

The line moved forward.

"Perfume might be nice," Kendall said. "Or a fiancé. If you had one of those I could be a flower girl finally."

Carly smiled. "Perfume might be an easier order for Santa to fill and it will fit into my stocking. Though I appreciate the other sugges-tions."

"Especially the fiancé," Kendall said.

Carly didn't want to get into that discussion.

Boyfriends and fiancés meant more complications. She had enough right now. She caught Jake's eye, and her stomach tingled.

Darn him.

"Do you know what you want Santa to bring you, Uncle Jake?" Austin asked him.

"Not yet, but I still have a few minutes to figure it out."

"Better hurry," she said.

His lips curved into a slow, easy grin. "I don't like rushing."

A devilish gleam filled his eyes, hinting at things she could only fantasize about. Forget the snow outside, she suddenly felt hot.

"But I'll think of something. I don't want to miss out on a candy cane," he added.

Peppermint kisses, anyone?

She sipped her drink. "This smoothie really hits the spot."

One of Santa's elves, a young woman wearing a floppy hat, green costume, red-and-white-striped tights and pointy-toed shoes with bells on them, took their photo order. Kendall and Austin sat on Santa's lap. Another female elf told the kids to smile and snapped pictures. After the third flash, Carly lost track of the number of photos taken. Santa asked the kids what they wanted and gave each one a candy cane.

"It's my aunt's turn," Austin announced.

Santa motioned her over.

Carly gulped. This was the last thing she had expected or wanted, especially with the long line of children waiting behind her and Jake watching her.

Santa patted space next to him. "Come sit and tell me what you want for Christmas, Carly."

She sat on the arm of his chair, feeling self-conscious. "I just came for a candy cane."

"You have to believe," Santa said.

"I gave up believing a long time ago," Carly muttered, too low for the children or Jake to hear. Six long years ago, when her love and her hopes had died on the mountain.

"Still, there must be something you want," Santa said.

She caught her gaze lingering on Jake and looked away. "No, thanks. Too risky."

The mall Santa must have followed her glance. "Life is about taking risks…and love makes those risks worth it even if we end up disappointed or hurt."

Carly thought she would fall off the chair arm in embarrassment. "I'm not looking for love," she assured him.

Especially not with Jake.

"Ah, but love may come looking for you,"

Santa said. With a warm smile, he handed her a candy cane.

She ducked her head as she accepted it. "I don't think so."

As she stood, Carly noticed Jake watching her. Surely he hadn't heard her. His cell phone rang, and he answered it.

"One more thing before you go." Santa kept his voice low. "You used to enjoy the holidays so much. There's no reason you can't feel that way again. All you have to do is give Christmas another chance."

"How—?"

"It's Uncle Jake's turn," Kendall said.

"Merry Christmas," Santa said.

Carly walked to the cashier in a daze. She looked over the pictures of the kids with Santa, picked one and paid her money.

What was going on? When did mall Santas decide to dispense advice along with candy canes?

Not that she was going to listen to him. Carly knew better than to take risks. That was one reason she had wanted to keep her distance from Jake Porter. The guy had heartbreak written all over him.

And why would she want to give Christmas another chance? She was willing to do what it took for the kids' sake, but that was all. That was enough.

Besides, no seasonal mall hire could possibly understand what she'd been through. Who was that guy anyway? Take away the red suit and the glasses and…he still looked like a perfectly cast Santa.

Coincidence. That was all. He'd made a lucky guess. No reason to be baffled or bothered by what he'd said.

Carly followed the path out of the North Pole Village. The kids stood with Jake, who held a candy cane in one hand, his cell phone in the other.

"Garrett called," Jake said.

"Is my mommy okay?" Austin asked.

Carly drew the two kids close to her.

"Absolutely," Jake said. "She and the baby are fine."

"Baby?" Carly held her breath.

"By C-section."

Something must have gone wrong. No doubt there was a story behind Hannah's needing an operation to deliver the baby, but the kids didn't need to hear it.

"So do I have a brother?" Austin asked.

"Or a sister?" Kendall asked.

"A brother," Jake announced. "It's a boy."

CHAPTER SIX

AT THE HOSPITAL, Jake walked with Carly to the gift shop. The bounce in her step brought a smile to his face. She hadn't seemed this happy at the mall.

"Isn't he the cutest baby?" Carly gushed about her new nephew even though she'd seen him for all of five minutes before letting the family have alone time together. "He looks like Hannah. Well, around the mouth. I think he has Garrett's chin."

"And his hair," Jake joked, shortening the length of his stride so Carly wouldn't have to hurry to keep up with him. Garrett was starting to go bald.

She continued as if Jake hadn't spoken, still on some kind of weird baby high. "Tyler Michael Willingham is a great name."

"It's an okay name, but Tyler Jacob Willingham would have been better. They could have called the kid T.J."

Her mouth quirked. "You do know Michael is Garrett's grandfather's and father's name, don't you?"

Jake shrugged, happy he'd made her smile. "Guys don't talk about names much."

"Not unless they are female names. I remember how you and Nick used to talk about girls."

"We only said those things because we knew you were listening." He laughed at her shocked expression. "Come on. Did you really think we didn't know when you were spying on us?"

She pursued her lips, making them look even more kissable than ever. "And I thought I was so clever."

"You were, but we were more clever."

Mischief gleamed in her eyes. "At least you told yourselves that."

As he laughed, a warm feeling built up inside him. He hadn't seen her in years, but since her return they had picked up right where they'd left off. Jake didn't know too many people he could do that with. "I'm glad you're back. I've missed you, Carly Bishop."

"Me, too," she said. "You, I mean."

She stumbled over her words as if she were tongue-tied or embarrassed, the way she'd done when she was a young girl. Years ago, Jake hadn't known why, but he liked thinking he might be the reason today. He stood taller. Each thing she did, every word she said, made him want to learn more about the woman she'd become while living in Philadelphia.

An elderly man pushed a gray-haired woman in a wheelchair toward them. His bony fingers wrapped tightly around the handgrips, and he took short, careful steps.

Carly moved to the right side of the hallway. Jake followed her, noticing the way her jeans fit. The couple passed by.

She stared after them. "The way that woman placed her hand on his was so sweet."

He'd missed it.

"I used to want to be like that," she said wistfully.

"Old and gnarled?"

She gave him a look. "I meant in love."

Jake shrugged. Love came with too many strings. People wanting him to change or be something he wasn't. At least that had been his experience with his parents and with women, but he wasn't about to discourage Carly. "All you need is to find the right guy and in fifty years you could be like them."

"You make it sound so easy."

"It could be if you keep your eyes open. He might be closer than you think."

Especially if he was right here with you now.

Whoa. Where had that come from?

Carly drew her brows together as if confused.

That made two of them.

He liked her kisses. He liked her. But the next fifty years… Jake rubbed the back of his neck. He was used to thinking in days or weeks, not years.

"What I mean is don't close yourself off to the possibility of meeting the right guy or you could miss out," Jake clarified.

"I'll take that into consideration." She stepped around an empty gurney. "So are you as happy as Austin that Hannah had a boy?"

He was happy Carly had changed the subject. "Boy or girl, doesn't matter. I'll have this one on skis before he can walk."

"How can you ski if you can't walk?" she asked.

"I'm sure if he can stand, there's a way," he said. "And if not, I'll load Tyler into a pack and ski with him on my back."

Carly raised her eyebrows. "You think Hannah's going to allow this?"

"She might mellow with baby number three."

"She's always been overprotective."

"I'm embracing the glass-half-full approach to life."

"I haven't figured out what my approach to life is yet," Carly admitted. "One day at a time has been my motto."

"Nothing wrong with that."

"That's what I keep telling myself." She stopped in front of the gift shop. "So what do you think? A stuffed animal and flowers?"

"I bought the baby a polar bear, but another kind of animal might be nice."

"Let's see what they have." Carly walked into the store, stopped and turned. Her smile lit up her entire face. "You bought Kendall and Austin bears."

Her remembering pleased Jake. "Kids like bears."

Carly nodded. "It's a very special tradition you started. Both Austin and Kendall still sleep with those bears on their beds. I'm sure Tyler will be no different once he's old enough."

"Each kid is different."

"You sound so much like a dad."

"Nope," he said. "Just a guy who watches kids every now and then."

"Just a guy, huh?" She shook her head. "I think one stuffed animal is enough for a newborn."

"Yes, but flowers for the new mommy are a must."

"So Hannah gets flowers even though it's not a date," Carly teased.

The dinner conversation at the Italian café came back to him. "Dates are only one time I bring flowers. Hospital visits are another," he explained. "But tomorrow I want to bring a small tree with lights and decorations. They can't spend Christmas in the hospital without a tree." He noticed the blank stare on Carly's face. "Hannah had a C-section like Tim Moreno's wife. That means she's going to be in the hospital for a few extra days. She won't be home for Christmas Eve or Christmas Day."

Carly's face paled. "I didn't even think of that. The kids—"

"Will be fine," he said. "Remember what we told Hannah."

"The best Christmas ever." Uncertainty filled Carly's voice.

"We will make this happen."

"We? I really appreciate all the help, but you have the brewery and your own family—"

"Stop." Jake stared into her eyes. "I've got the brewery under control no matter what my father thinks. And second, you guys are my family. Why would I want to spend Christmas in some fancy hotel eating overpriced food and being told I bought the wrong gift cards for my parents when I could be having fun with all of you?"

"Well, when you put it that way." Carly's tone was light, but she wasn't smiling. "Don't your parents miss you?"

"Not really. They liked the idea of having a child more than having a real child. Besides, I'll never live up to my father's expectations so not being around him much saves us from arguing more."

Compassion filled her eyes. "I'm sorry."

"No worries," he said, not wanting her pity. "It's the way things turned out. But at least now you know I'll be here to help. That's what friends are for."

"Thanks."

"Anytime." He wanted to reach out and touch her, but controlled the impulse. "You can always count on me, Carly. Don't ever forget that."

That night at the house, Carly laid out rolls of wrapping paper. The kids, exhausted from their busy day, were already sound asleep. She wondered how much sleep she'd manage tonight.

Jake carried a large black plastic bag full of

items into the living room. She stared at the muscles beneath his shirt. Definite hard body. "This is the last of the presents."

"I don't know what I would do without you."

"Pretty indispensable, huh?" he asked.

"In some instances."

Carly didn't like that. She depended on one person only—herself. It was easier that way. Less complicated. And yet she couldn't have given the kids the Christmas they deserved on her own. She needed Jake. His help, that was.

He set the bag next to the others he'd brought down from the attic. "What next?"

A nervous breakdown.

Carly realized she was crunching a roll of blue-and-white snowflake wrapping paper. She loosened her grip and set the roll on the floor. She struggled to hold herself together, feeling as if she were about to unravel. She'd gone eight rounds with Christmas today, and felt emotionally raw. But it wasn't only the holidays she'd been battling. She'd been fighting her feelings for Jake, too.

She hadn't felt this vulnerable in years. The conflict inside her was talking its toll. If Jake knew how she was feeling, she'd be in big trouble.

"Nothing," she answered finally.

Best to send him on his way before he figured it out, or worse, she threw herself into his arms and couldn't let go.

Carly had a late, emotional night ahead of her. A box of tissues and chocolates were definitely in order along with the wrapping paper, ribbons and bows.

"Tomorrow's going to be a busy day." She placed the scissors and rolls of tape on the coffee table. "Go home and get some sleep."

He stood tall, his shoulders squared, as if he were ready to go to battle himself. "I'm not going anywhere."

She fought a rush of panic. "The brewery—"

"Manages without me when I go on a mission. It's no big deal if I don't stop in tonight. Don't forget, I'm a phone call away if they need me."

"You've done so much already. Talk about going above and beyond."

"You've done just as much. And look at all this." He motioned to the bags of presents. "You can't wrap all of this on your own."

"I can." She had to. Because however tired she was physically, emotionally, doing it on her own was better than continuing to rely on him for help.

"If I leave, you'll be up all night." He removed a box from one of the bags, his long fingers wrapping around a board game. "I'm not going to do that to you."

She needed him to leave her. Now. "I appreciate the offer, but I don't mind."

"I do."

The fire crackled. The wind blew outside. Carly could think of a million other places she'd rather be at the moment, but she was stuck here. She needed to be alone.

"Jake—"

"I know what's missing." He walked to the stereo and fiddled with the radio dial. "We can't do this without setting the mood."

Carly's heart slammed against her chest. Dread filled her.

He wouldn't.

Except…she'd never told him about her discomfort with the whole Christmas season. She'd never told anyone except…Santa.

"Silent Night" played through the speakers.

She felt as if she might lose it any minute. Her shoulders sagged. "I'd rather we didn't have Christmas music playing."

He sorted the presents into stacks. One for Kendall. Another for Austin. "Why not?"

Carly took a deep breath, but didn't say anything. She couldn't say anything.

"Come on," he said. "Tell me."

"Christmas," she whispered as if it were some taboo word not supposed to be spoken. "I don't like it."

"Sure you do." He shot her a quizzical look as he placed a snowboard in Austin's pile. "You love Christmas. More than anyone I know."

She shook her head.

He froze. "You're serious?"

"Completely serious."

"But you used to bake all those cookies and spend hours decorating them with icing and candies. You'd make people gifts each year. And I'll never forget those Christmas carols you played all the time. Nick and I used to make up stupid lyrics to go with the music so you would turn them off."

Jake and Nick had irritated her so much with their words and singing, but she had only turned up the volume when they did that.

"That was before," she admitted. "I—I don't celebrate Christmas anymore. I haven't since I moved to Philadelphia."

"The accident."

It wasn't a question. She nodded, grateful for his instant understanding. "I found it difficult, okay, impossible, to separate the accident from Christmas. Especially after the Christmas Eve wedding that wasn't. The feelings of guilt were so strong they threatened to suffocate me every time December rolled around. So I stopped celebrating Christmas. No one knew then. Or knows now."

His assessing gaze make her self-conscious. "You send gifts."

"I shop for presents all year-round, wrap them in September and package them so they're ready to mail after Thanksgiving. But now with Hannah in the hospital over Christmas I fear my secret is going to get out."

"Your secret is safe with me."

His words wrapped around her heart. She trusted he wouldn't say anything. "Thank you."

"Today must have been hard for you."

"I did what I had to do."

"You did a great job." He opened his arms. Carly went cautiously, but the moment he embraced her, she knew it was exactly what she needed. What she'd been wanting all night long. His hug offered comfort, strength and understanding. "Tell me what you need to get you through this and it's yours."

You.

What she needed was him. Uh-oh. She sure couldn't tell him that.

"Thanks," she said, not knowing what else to say.

"You know, maybe having to do Christmas for the kids will bring back your love of the holiday."

"That's not possible."

"Anything's possible," he said. "The Grinch figured out the meaning of Christmas in a night."

"And I thought you calling me a pest was bad." She crinkled her nose. "Now you're comparing me to the Grinch?"

"It's either him or Ebenezer Scrooge. Don't forget he learned what Christmas meant in a night, too."

This must be Jake's glass-half-full approach. She sighed. "I already know the meaning of Christmas. I just choose not to do anything about it."

"Be careful what you say."

"Why is that?" Carly asked.

He winked. "Because I'm always up for a challenge."

Forget about loving a challenge.

After four hours of wrapping, tagging and tying ribbons, Jake understood a little better why Carly felt the way she did about Christmas. But he wasn't about to give up. On the holiday or her.

She needed him. More than he'd realized. All he had to do was make her see it, too.

"That was harder than I thought it would be." Give him a length of rope, and he could tie one-handed bowlines with his eyes closed, but he couldn't tie a pretty bow around a present to save his life. "Good thing you were here to tie those ribbons."

"Well, I'm relieved you took the presents up to the attic. That was the last thing to check off my list for today." She sat on the couch, her legs curled underneath her and her eyes closed. "Do you think it would be bad if I slept here tonight?"

Not if he could join her. Oops. Wrong answer. He tried again. "It might get cold without a blanket."

"True, but I have the fire to keep me warm."

"Not unless you plan to keep stoking it so the fire burns all night."

"Stop." She yawned and covered her mouth. "It's too late for reality."

Jake was up for a little fantasy himself. He wanted to give Carly whatever she wanted.

"It's not too late for what I have in mind," he said.

"What is that?" she asked.

"Be right back."

"Take your time," she mumbled. "Please."

Jake returned a few minutes later. He set two

glasses of eggnog on the coffee table. "This might make you feel better and give you enough strength to make it to your bed."

Carly's eyes sprang open. She saw the drinks and smiled. "Oh, this might give me the second wind I need. Is that nutmeg on top?"

"Freshly ground just for you."

Her warm, sleepy eyes brightened. "You are amazing."

He smiled at the compliment. "So are you."

Carly raised her glass to him. "To being amazing tonight."

"I'll drink to that." Jake sat next to her, picked up his glass and tapped it against hers. "Cheers."

She took a sip. "Delicious."

"Eggnog," he said. "A tasty Christmas tradition."

"This is one tradition I still enjoy." She took another sip. "See, I'm not the Grinch or a Scrooge."

"True." The carols playing in the background no longer seemed to bother her. "We could try another tradition to make sure."

"What do you have in mind?" she asked.

"Mistletoe?"

She laughed. "In your dreams."

Not quite the reaction he was hoping for, but

at least she seemed more relaxed now. Jake wanted the joy back in her eyes. The way it had been at the hospital earlier.

He fought the urge to take her in his arms and hold her. To give her comfort, hugs, whatever she needed. But he couldn't. The line between friend and something more was already blurring. He needed Carly to give him a sign she was ready for more.

So he sat next to her, ignoring his need to touch her, to kiss her.

"You've been listening to Christmas music for the past four hours. It's time to sing along."

"I don't sing."

"That's true. I remember a couple of your Backstreet Boys renditions."

She swatted his arm. "Hey."

"Kidding." Jake laughed. He listened to the song playing on the radio. "I'm sure you remember the words to 'Jingle Bells.'"

"I could probably hum along…"

"That's the spirit."

"…if you got me a cookie."

"The ghost of Christmas present just rolled over in his grave."

She grinned. "Can I have his cookie, too?"

He tickled her side.

Carly erupted into laughter. She tried to

tickle him back, but he arched his body away from her. "No fair. You're bigger than me."

"Older and wiser, too."

"Older, yes." Amusement gleamed in her eyes. "But wiser?"

He tickled her more, until their bodies touched and their faces were mere inches apart. Her full lips drew his attention. He wanted to kiss her.

Instead he let go of her and moved back to his spot on the couch. A wise move? Time would tell, but it felt like the right move.

"I'm going home," he said. "I'll pick you guys up in the morning. We can get a tree and take it to the hospital."

"Sounds good."

"I have to be at work tomorrow afternoon," he said. "We're having a Christmas Eve buffet. Why don't you and the kids come?"

"That would be great. Hannah ordered a meal that only needs to be heated for Christmas dinner, but I hadn't figured out what to do for tomorrow night."

"I'll pick you up."

"You have to work."

"It won't take me that long to swing by."

"Okay," she said. "The kids will like that."

Jake was more interested in whether or not she was looking forward to seeing him again so soon, but he wasn't sure she was ready for the question—or that he was ready for the answer. He stood and walked to the front door. "See you tomorrow morning."

Carly nodded. "Jake."

He turned.

She stood, her eyes serious. "Thanks for everything. I appreciate all your help, but it was, um, really great having you here tonight. And not just to help me with stuff."

Her sincere words filled him with warmth. Jake smiled. He might not have gotten to kiss her tonight, but he would get his chance again.

Maybe sooner than he expected.

In thirty-six hours, Christmas would be behind her for another year. Carly couldn't wait. At least the day hadn't been too painful so far. Thanks to Jake.

She forced herself not to look at him. Not an easy thing in Hannah's cozy hospital room. But Carly had been staring and thinking about him too much. He'd become a part of her daily life, but she wasn't about to let him under her skin. Or into her heart.

Austin hung a silver bell on the small live tree they'd bought this morning. "This is so much fun."

The fresh fir scent and new baby smell masked the sterile hospital aroma Carly had smelled yesterday. And with all the noise—talking, laughter and Kendall's boot heels clicking against the tile floor—it seemed more like a party than hospital visit. "Christmas Eve should be fun."

"We've never decorated a tree on Christmas Eve before," Kendall said.

"That's because it's tradition to put up our tree on the first Sunday of December," Hannah said from her hospital bed. She hadn't stopped smiling or watching her kids since they arrived. She looked too rested to have given birth yesterday. "This one, however, is a very special tree. We'll plant it in the yard so it can grow with Tyler."

As Carly added hooks to the ornaments they'd purchased that morning, Austin removed a gold ball from the box.

"We can see who grows taller. Tyler or the tree," Jake said.

Carly glanced his way. He stood with the baby in his arms. Her breath caught in her throat. Her heart skipped at least two beats.

Talk about a natural. Okay, Jake had held Kendall and Austin as babies, but Carly remembered how he'd been back then. A little awkward trying to support the baby's head, but Jake's method couldn't be critiqued now.

An image of him holding his own child formed in Carly's mind. A beautiful child with the same piercing blue eyes and killer smile. A child that was hers, too.

The thought made her heart pound and her pulse race. Until she realized what she was daydreaming about.

Carly couldn't think of Jake as a father let alone the father of her baby. She'd given up on that dream. For now at least. And with Jake. A relationship with him could jeopardize the special place he held within this family. Not to mention the risk to her heart. She wet her dry lips.

"Babies can only see black, red and white," Garrett said.

"Not this baby." Jake's tone spoke of a deep affection for the child he held in his arms.

Austin nodded. "Our baby is the smartest baby. And he doesn't smell bad."

"At least not yet," Hannah muttered. "Come over here."

Carly sat on the chair next to the bed, noticing the photograph of the kids with Santa already set on her rolling bed tray.

"The kids are so happy being with you and Jake."

Hannah made them sound like a couple. Carly shifted in her seat. "It's been fun."

"I don't know how to thank you."

"No thanks are necessary. I'm having fun myself." Her gaze strayed to Jake. She forced her attention back to Hannah. "Don't worry about a thing. It's all being taken care of."

"What about you? Are doing okay?" Hannah asked, curiosity dripping from each word.

"I'm fine."

"You sure about that?" Hannah lowered her voice. "You and Jake seem sort of, well, chummy."

"We're friends," Carly whispered, ignoring the fact they'd kissed. She'd been trying hard to forget what had happened the other day. "That's all."

Hannah's eyes clouded with concern. "You're sure that's all?"

"Being friends is enough." After Carly had said the words, a part of her—the same part that liked when he pulled her into his arms and held her last night—wondered if that were true. She'd once liked the boy. She didn't have too many complaints about the man. Face it, men like Jacob Porter weren't easy to find.

But…the complications.

She had too much to lose if things went

wrong. So did Hannah and the kids. Even Garrett. Carly wasn't willing to take the chance.

"Way more than enough," she added.

Hannah gave her a dubious look. The same one she'd given when Iain proposed and Carly had wanted a short engagement so they could marry on Christmas Eve.

"Just be careful," Hannah whispered. "I love Jake to death. I know he cares about you and has for a long time, but he doesn't exactly have the best track record when it comes to relationships. The last thing I want is for you to be hurt."

"I don't want that, either," Carly admitted. "I promise I'll be careful."

So careful she wouldn't have the opportunity to get hurt, let alone kiss Jake again.

CHAPTER SEVEN

THAT AFTERNOON after Jake had dropped them at home, Kendall and Austin decorated sugar cookies shaped like snowmen, stars, reindeer, candy canes, stockings and angels. The stove beeped. Carly turned off the timer. "The final batch is ready."

"They smell so good," Austin said.

The scent of freshly baked cookies filled her nostrils, bringing back memories of the Christmases that had come before. "They're almost better than gingerbread."

"We've never made gingerbread," Kendall said.

"You have." Six years ago. When Nick had still been alive. But that was the last time Carly had been with them at Christmastime. Her parents, too, since they'd moved after their divorce. "You were little, though."

And wouldn't have remembered.

That hurt. And yet, Garrett and Hannah, even Jake, couldn't be blamed for not honoring that particular Bishop tradition. It probably never even crossed their minds. But now all the things Nick loved growing up were unfamiliar to his children.

That wasn't fair to them. Or Nick.

Carly needed to fix that. "Your daddy and I always made a gingerbread house at Christmastime."

"I want to make one," Austin said.

"There isn't time tonight and we'll be at the hospital most of Christmas, but the next day I'll show you all you need to know about gingerbread, okay?"

Kendall beamed. "I can't wait."

"Me, either," Austin said.

Carly placed the cookies on a cooling rack. "That makes three of us."

"Four of us if you count Uncle Jake," Kendall added. "He'll want to help. Especially if food's involved."

Carly wouldn't mind Jake being there. She wiped her hands on the Mrs. Claus apron she wore. He'd been the one thing missing this afternoon. She kept thinking he should be here.

The song "I'll Be Home for Christmas" played on the radio. She listened to the lyrics, mentally composing a list like one Hannah had given her.

Snow, check.

Mistletoe, check.

Presents under the tree, check.

Not bad. Add in baking cookies and Carly was doing pretty good. Granted, this might not qualify as the best Christmas ever, but things were definitely better than she had expected.

Jake would be pleased.

Not that she wanted to please him. Carly placed the cookie sheet in the sink. Okay, maybe a little.

Uh-oh. She couldn't forget her promise to Hannah about being careful. Yet here Carly was, missing Jake. Wanting to please him. Becoming attached to him. Not smart. Carly washed the cookie sheet. The last thing she wanted to get was burned.

Austin popped a few candy sprinkles into his mouth. "Santa's going to love these cookies, Aunt Carly."

"Yes, he will." She pointed to the red candies on the snowman's chest. "I like how you used cinnamon candies for his buttons."

Kendall tilted her chin. "It was my idea."

"Was not," Austin said.

"Was, too."

Carly whistled. Both kids stopped talking. "It's Christmas Eve. Santa still has time to take gifts off his sleigh."

The kids exchanged worried glances.

She looked at them both. "Let's concentrate on decorating the cookies and not arguing with each other, okay?"

Kendall and Austin placed new cookies in front of them and set to work.

"After we get home from dinner at the brewpub—" Carly placed candy sprinkles on the angel's wings she was decorating "—we can make a plate of cookies for Santa and one with carrots and celery for the reindeer."

Kendall's brow furrowed. "We've never left anything for the reindeer before."

Oh, Nick. I shouldn't have stayed away so long. Forgive me.

"Your daddy taught me to leave treats for the reindeer when I was a little girl," Carly explained. "Don't forget, Santa visits a lot of houses tonight, but it's the reindeer who do all the flying. They deserve something to snack on, too."

Austin flashed her a grin. "Will you come back next Christmas so we can do this all over again?"

Both kids stared expectantly at her. Carly

took a deep breath. "I would love to come back, but we need to talk to your parents first."

"Oh, they won't mind." Kendall piped a red ball of icing on the end of a reindeer's nose. "Mommy always says she wishes you lived closer."

Carly stared at the angel cookie in front of her. "Sometimes I wish that, too."

"Then move," Austin said. "This is the best place to live in the entire world."

"Philadelphia's not too bad," she countered.

Austin looked at her as if she'd lost her mind. "But we're not there."

She thought about his words. The kids weren't there. Neither was Jake. But she hadn't been trying to escape them, only the mountain, a constant reminder of all she'd lost. "You're right about that."

They continued decorating cookies. Time seemed to fly. The sprinkles and colored sugars disappeared. Only a dab of icing remained.

"Do you hear that, Aunt Carly?" Kendall asked.

Carly realized she was humming along to the catchy Christmas carol spilling from the radio. Uh-oh. She wet her lips. "Hear what?"

Kendall pursed her lips. "Jingle bells."

"'Deck the Halls,'" Carly corrected.

"Not on the radio, silly! Listen."

She listened and heard a faint jingling in the distance. "You're right. It's not the radio."

"I hear it, too." Austin pushed his chair back from the table and stood. He looked up and down and all around. "Maybe one of Santa's elves is checking to see if we're being good."

"You never know," Carly said. "Or one of the inns or resorts is offering sleigh rides tonight."

"I wish we could go on a sleigh ride," Kendall said with a wistful tone.

The longing in her niece's voice made Carly want to flag down the sleigh right then and there. She might not be in a position to make Kendall a flower girl, but this was something Carly could give her. "We could find out how much a sleigh ride costs and see if they are doing them after Christmas."

Kendall grinned. "That would be so cool."

"Very cool." Carly just hoped she could afford it. Seeing the look in the little girl's eyes, she almost didn't care.

"Did you ever go on a sleigh ride?" Kendall asked.

"No," Carly admitted.

Kendall's face fell.

"I went on a dog sled ride once, though," Carly offered. She had begged and begged for years, but her parents always said it was too expensive.

Austin stopped munching on a broken candy-cane-shaped cookie. "When?"

Carly remembered the wind in her face as the team drove around Frog Lake one chilly afternoon. She'd helped care for the dogs afterward. "When I was fifteen."

"Did your aunt take you?"

She laughed. "No, it was a special present from your daddy and…Uncle Jake."

Her brother had given her the gift, but Jake had played a role in the present. She suspected he might even have helped Nick pay for it.

"Uncle Jake gives the best presents," Kendall said.

"He does." The best kisses, too. Carly touched her lips with her fingertips. Careful. She knew more kisses were a really bad idea, but her lips seemed to disagree. Still she wasn't about to have a fling during her winter vacation and risk losing Jake's friendship forever.

And her heart again.

Austin cupped his ear with his hand. "Listen. The bells are getting closer."

Kendall ran to the living-room window. Austin followed at her heels. Carly took up the rear.

"It's on our street," Kendall said. "Coming to our house."

The kids pressed their noises against the glass and sighed.

"Look at the horse." Wonder filled Austin's voice.

Carly looked out the window. A large, black horse pulled a red sleigh hung with garlands. Two bright lanterns bobbed at the front. A driver, wearing an old-fashioned stovepipe hat on his head and a cape around his shoulders, held on to the reins. "Do you see anyone besides the driver?"

"Uncle Jake," the two said at the same time. They jumped and shrieked.

Who else but Uncle Jake? A warm and fuzzy feeling flowed through Carly. The only things missing were chestnuts roasting and carolers decked out in Victorian clothing. "He said he would pick us up, but I had no idea this was what he had in mind. Come on, guys, let's get ready."

As the kids washed and changed clothes, Carly threw away what little icing remained, snapped the lids back on the cookie decorations, washed her hands and removed her apron.

The doorbell rang. She smiled. Perfect timing.

"Merry Christmas," Jake said.

Her heart expanded. His cheeks were ruddy with cold, but his blue eyes were so warm.

"It's not Christmas yet," Kendall said.

"True, but it will be in a few hours," he said, looking stylish and handsome in his blue down jacket, olive-green pants and fleece hat. "That's why I thought a sleigh ride tonight might be a fun way to go to dinner."

Austin jumped up and down. "It'll be the funnest way ever."

"Thank you, Uncle Jake." Kendall hugged him. "I bet no one else gets to do this."

"Let's go, let's go," Austin sang.

Carly felt a tingle as she watched the scene in front of her. The kids' love and gratitude for Jake was just as strong as his for them. Lucky kids. But someone had to be practical. "Get on your coats, hats and mittens."

"What smells so good?" Jake asked.

"We baked cookies for Santa," Kendall said. "You can have one."

"I can't wait. Thanks." He looked at Carly and grinned. "Nothing like making Christmas cookies on Christmas Eve to put you in the holiday spirit."

Austin struggled with her zipper. "We're going to make gingerbread houses, too."

"Our daddy used to make it," Kendall added, jamming a hat over her blond curls.

"I didn't know that," Jake admitted.

"A Bishop family tradition," she replied.

"Maybe I could learn, too," he said.

"Sure." She shrugged into her jacket. "Thanks for arranging the sleigh ride. It's exactly what the kids need."

His gaze locked on hers. "I didn't do this only for the kids."

Her heart bumped. Had he done this for her? "Oh. Well…"

"We couldn't all fit into a dog sled. I figured a sleigh was the next best thing."

His thoughtfulness, his teasing, warmed her from the inside out. And so did the look in his eyes. "The best," she corrected. "Thanks."

"You're welcome." His smile widened. "Are you ready to go?"

At that moment, she would have followed him anywhere. Not trusting what she might say, Carly nodded.

"Hop on the sleigh, kids," he said.

Kendall and Austin ran outside, their footsteps crunching on the snow. Their laughter was a perfect complement to the jingle bells on the horse's harnesses.

Carly watched them. "The kids are so excited."

"What about you?" Jake asked.

A beat passed. She didn't dare look at him. "I'm pretty excited, too."

"The fun is only beginning."

Anticipation filled her. With the one-horse open sleigh in the driveway surrounded by all the snow-covered trees and delicate snowflakes falling from the sky, she felt as if she'd stepped into a greeting card.

Outside, the cold air tasted like…Christmas. She smelled snow, pine and smoke from fireplaces. By the time she crossed the driveway, Kendall and Austin were sitting on either side of the sleigh driver. Carly could see their breaths, but the low temperatures didn't seem to bother them one bit. Still, Jake covered the kids with thick blankets.

Carly sat on the padded seat in the back. He joined her, his thigh pressing against hers.

He spread a blanket over her. "Warm enough?"

Any warmer and her blood would boil. "Very cozy, thank you."

"Well, if you get cold, I know how to warm you up."

She wondered what he had in mind.

As the sleigh glided forward, the horse's bells jingled, almost drowning out the kids' conversation with the driver. Carly removed her camera from her purse and took a picture of them.

"They'll remember this forever," she confided with a smile.

Jake looked uncomfortable. "I don't know about forever. I just want them to enjoy tonight."

"They will. They are." She lowered the camera to her lap. "And if they ever forget tonight, they'll have a photo to help them remember. I still have a picture of me with those sled dogs. Did I ever thank you for that?"

"The sled ride was mostly Nick's present."

"But it was your idea," she guessed.

"Big deal." Jake took the camera from her and snapped her picture. The flash made her see spots. "Going on a dog sled ride for your birthday was all you talked about from the time you were ten. It didn't take much imagination to know it was time to make it happen."

"But—"

"Smile." He held the camera out in front of the two of them and leaned his head against hers. The flash blinded her again.

She blinked. "What nineteen-year-old guy would go to so much trouble?"

"A guy who realized his best friend's sister

was growing up to be a beautiful young woman."

Carly's cheeks warmed.

Jake tucked a strand of hair back into her hat. The gesture was intimate, but felt so right.

"You're even more beautiful now, Carly."

Heaven help her. She forced herself to take a deep breath. "You're really determined to make this the best Christmas ever, aren't you?"

The festive atmosphere in the brewpub couldn't have been more perfect. The place was packed. Miniature lights around the bar flashed on and off. Small red foil-covered pots of poinsettias sat on each table. The fireplace crackled with a burning blaze. Conversations drowned out the Christmas carols playing on the sound system, but no one seemed to care. A few hardy souls at one table sang carols on their own. And the mouthwatering scent of the buffet had patrons thinking more about the tasty food than the beer on tap.

Jake couldn't be happier. No doubt his father would find something to complain about, but his father wasn't here to dampen his mood.

Satisfaction filled Jake as he stared from behind the bar at Carly and the kids eating dinner. All three were smiling and laughing. Fun times. Just as he'd hoped.

He would return to the table once things settled down, but he needed to help his bartender keep up with orders right now. He handed a server three glasses—two porters and an ale.

"Why don't you take a picture of her," a familiar male voice said. "It'll last longer."

Jake didn't look up. As he filled a pint-size glass with Nick's Winter Ale, he thought about what Carly had said on the sleigh ride.

And if they ever forget tonight, they'll have a photo to help them remember.

What was he going to have when this was over? A picture of Carly and a few memories? Or a whole lot of regrets?

Jake set the drink on the bar. "Merry Christmas, Sean."

"Same to you." Sean Hughes sat on the bar stool and raised his glass. "To Nick. Wherever you are, my friend, climb on."

Jake lifted his water glass into the air. "Hear, hear."

Sean glanced back at Carly and the kids. "You finally putting the moves on her?"

Jake clenched his jaw. "Thinking about it."

"You've been going to an awful lot of trouble for her."

"Not just for her. The kids, too." Jake placed his glass back under the bar. It hadn't felt like trouble to him. "I'm only doing what needs to be done."

Sean swirled the beer in his glass. "Is that what's best for Carly?"

"Since when do you offer dating advice?" Jake asked, filling another Nick's Winter Ale and two pale ales.

Sean shrugged. "Nick would be saying the same stuff to you if he were here."

"If Nick were here, he would have punched me out as soon as he found out I'd kissed Carly."

"True, that," Sean said. "I can punch you for him if it would make you feel better."

Jake handed a server two pints of amber. "Thanks, but no thanks."

Sean took another swig of his beer. "Just remember she's still Nick's little sister. Not some flavor of the month."

"I know that." But saying those words made the fact sink in.

"Thanks for the beer." Sean took a large swig. "Better get back to the parents' house before Denali starts wondering where I've been."

"Denali is a dog."

"She's still a female." Sean downed the rest of his glass. "See you tomorrow."

"Looking forward to it." Jake filled another order, but his mind was on something else. Someone else. Nick.

Sean raised a good point.

What would Nick Bishop think about Jake wanting to be with Carly? He glanced at her and rubbed his jaw. Jake didn't think he wanted to know the answer.

Four hours later, Carly watched Jake. He sat in the middle of the living-room floor surrounded by pirate ship pieces. Frustration coupled with intense concentration creased his forehead. The look totally contradicted the carefree, almost messy style of his hair. Hair she wanted to brush her fingers through.

Oops. That wasn't being careful. Or smart.

Time to put the brakes on whatever attraction she was feeling. Physical attraction, she amended. When she returned to Philadelphia after New Year's, Jake would be out of sight. That would put him out of her mind and she'd be back to normal.

"You need a mechanical engineering degree to get the damn thing out of the box." He twisted the wire securing the hull to a piece of cardboard. "Forget about the packaging being kid-proof. This thing is fully adult-proof."

"I should have wrapped the box instead."

"And put this together on Christmas day with Austin standing over me asking every two minutes when it'll be ready to play with?" Jake succeeded in removing the last piece. "No way. I've done this enough times to know better."

"I feel like a total newbie," Carly admitted. "When the kids were younger, the presents were less complicated. A rocking horse, a toy box, a ride-on car."

"I remember those days." He held two ship parts in his hands. "But you seem to know what you're doing."

"Hannah's list." Carly arranged the presents under the tree. "Between that and you, I've had all I needed."

He gazed up at her. "Flattery will get you everywhere."

"I'll have to remember that."

"Just so you know. Being with you has been great." The way his eyes looked at her felt almost like a caress. "And I wouldn't have missed any of this. Christmas and kids go hand in hand. Wait until morning when Kendall and Austin run down the stairs, see the presents under the tree and scream at the top of their lungs."

"You must get here early to see all that."

He nodded. "Last year, Garrett and I took a long time putting together bikes for the kids so I ended up staying the night, but that made things easier in the morning. I didn't have to get up so early."

Easier in the morning, but what about bedtime?

The thought of saying good-night to Jake in the house alone filled her stomach with butterflies. Okay, they weren't totally alone, but their chaperones were fast asleep, dreaming about sugar plums, snowboards and the hottest new video game platform.

"I'm not fishing for an invitation if that's what you're worried about," he added.

"I didn't think you were. And I'm not worried." Darn. She sounded defensive. "I'm just not used to any of this."

"You mean, Christmas."

"Among other things." Like him.

"What other things?" he asked.

Carly blew out a breath. "I know we're just friends, but being with you these past couple of days has been like playing house."

His eyes gleamed. "You used to like playing house."

"I was eight, not twenty-eight," she said. "Everything has been so wonderful. Tonight was simply magical, but it's getting hard to tell what was pretend and what was real."

"It can be whatever you want it to be."

That's what she was afraid of. Part of her wanted it to be real, but that would mean taking chances again.

"You said it yourself, Carly. We're friends. We're having fun. It's Christmas Eve. Why don't we let whatever happens happen?"

The thought of doing what he suggested scared her. Carly didn't take chances, but she couldn't deny how wonderful being with Jake felt. It was as if a Christmas fairy had sprinkled magical snowflake dust on them. Maybe following his advice would be…okay.

Carly took a deep breath. "I—I can do that."

"Good." His smile reassured her. "Now want to help me put together this pirate ship so we can finish up everything?"

Relieved, disappointed, she nodded. "Where are the instructions?"

"I'm not big on instructions—" he reached under the box and pulled out a white booklet "—but you can use them."

She read the directions, found the necessary pieces and assembled the captain's quarter. "We might get the ship put together faster if we both followed the directions."

"I have a better idea." His eyes narrowed in on her. "Let's divide the ship parts in half. Whoever finishes first wins. You use the instructions. I won't. What do you say?"

The challenging tone of his voice reminded her of the bets Jake and Nick had made over the years, decades really. "I thought you would have outgrown making stupid bets by now."

"Nope. And they're not stupid bets." Jake set the pieces of the ship on the carpet. "Sean ended up having to chop my firewood this fall after we bet on how much rockfall we'd see. He then wanted to go double or nothing by guessing when the bergschrund would be open. He, of course, lost."

"He shouldn't have bet to start with." She glanced over the directions. "I'm not much of a gambler."

"Even if it's a sure thing?" he asked.

"Nothing's ever a sure thing." Carly knew that better than anybody. She picked up two new parts of the ship and studied at the diagram in the instruction manual. "Though I must admit I'm partial to guarantees."

"I see nothing wrong with a friendly wager every now and then."

How friendly? She snapped a rail onto the ship's deck. "That's because you rarely lose."

"Losing is always a possibility, but that's what makes it exciting."

Exciting? Try terrifying. "I don't think so."

All Carly had done for the past six years was lose. Her fiancé. Her brother. Her parents being together. Pretty much everything and everyone she'd grown up loving had disappeared or changed. Every person she'd loved had disappointed her. She couldn't take anything else.

"We could make the prize something easy," he suggested. "Whatever you want."

She wanted Jake to hold her, to pull her against him and kiss her. Hard. The thought alone raised her temperature ten degrees. Not good.

His flashed her a charming lopsided grin. "I'll give you a head start."

"Don't try to egg me into accepting a bet. I've already put more pieces together than you."

"Then you can't lose."

She wished that were the case, but experience had painted a much different picture with wide brush strokes even she couldn't pretend not to see. "No, thanks."

"You said you would let whatever happens happen."

Carly stared at him. "Are you always so…?"

He raised a brow. "Charming?"

"Persistent?"

Jake laughed. "It depends on how much I want something."

"And you want it, I mean a bet, this much."

"Yes—" the intensity in his eyes took her breath away "—I want…it that much."

Oh, boy. Anticipation skittered down her spine.

"What do you say, Carly? Will you take a chance?"

His smile full of warmth and laughter hinted at a promise she couldn't even imagine. A simple bet with an easy prize. She was tempted—oh, so tempted, considering she'd already agreed to let whatever happen happen.

"Come on," he urged, those baby blues of his melting away her resolve. "What have you got to lose?"

Only one thing, she realized. Her heart.

"I can't believe I lost the bet." Jake ate another cookie. He'd already munched down carrots and taken bites out of celery sticks before tossing them outside so the kids would think the reindeer had eaten them. "But if you thought drinking milk and eating cookies left for Santa would be a chore, it's not."

"Somebody had to do it." Carly lay on the

couch. "Better you than me. If I ate them, they'd go straight to my hips."

But they sure were nice hips. She had curves in all the right places.

"I'll do anything to help the cause." Jake bit into another cookie, a snowman with red candy buttons on his front.

"So you would have eaten the cookies even if you'd won the bet?" she asked.

"If you had wanted me to."

He wanted to help her. Not out of guilt, but because he cared. Not for the girl she'd been, but the woman she'd become.

Is that what's best for Carly?

Hell, yes. Jake only wanted what was best for her. Even if that might not be him.

A soft, sweet smile graced her lips, and Jake's heart did a flip-flop. "Thank you," she said.

"You're welcome, but are you sure you don't want something else from me?" He walked toward her. "You won fair and square, but I'm the one who got the treats."

"I'm good." She glanced at the clock. "I'm a little tired, but happy we got everything done before midnight."

"We're a good team."

She nodded.

Jake raised her sock-covered feet off the couch, sat and placed them on his lap. As he touched her left foot, she tensed. The moment he rubbed, the tension seeped from her body.

She sunk into the couch. "Oh, thank you."

"You deserve it," he said. "You've been on your feet all day."

"I'm on my feet at work."

"Yes, but you're not used to this kind of work."

"You're not kidding." Her eyelids closed. She sighed. "Is there anything Jake Porter can't do?"

"I suck at differential equations."

Her eyes remained closed. "When was the last time you did one of those?"

"On the final exam."

She smiled. "You're going to have to come up with something better than that."

He moved to the other foot.

"Oh, Jake." She practically purred. "This is wonderful."

He agreed. "Glad you're liking it."

"I'm loving it."

He wished he could give her more, but he didn't want to press his luck.

A cuckoo clock Nick had bought on a ski trip to Switzerland sounded twelve times. Midnight.

She opened her eyes and sat with her elbows supporting her weight on the sofa's armrest. "Merry Christmas."

"Merry Christmas, Carly."

A beat passed. And another.

Their eyes locked. Even their breathing seemed in sync.

What he wouldn't give for some mistletoe because if there ever was a perfect time for a kiss it was now.

Right now.

But Jake hesitated. He didn't want to make the wrong move. He'd known fear, on the mountain, not knowing if he'd make it down in one piece. The quiet. The waiting. The unknown.

Jake felt like that now.

Oh, the stakes weren't life or death, but they felt high nonetheless. What was the price of a kiss?

A brush of his lips on her forehead. A friendly peck on her cheek. A juicy one planted right on her lips. He wasn't about to be picky though if he had his choice he'd go for juicy. Especially if it was going to cost him. He rubbed her ankles.

If only he knew what she wanted him to do. Not that he had a clue himself beyond wanting a kiss. But the wanting alone pushed what he was feeling out of the friendship realm and into something else altogether. So he sat, his hands on her feet, holding his breath, waiting for inspiration to strike.

He'd told her to take a chance. Yet he was unable to do the same. Coward. He might as well plop down on a nest and warm a clutch of eggs.

Yawning, she stretched her arms above her head. "Sorry. It's been a long day."

"It's late, too," he said, breaking the mood like a glass dropped on a tile floor. "I should probably be going."

Carly moistened her lips. "Unless you want to stay the night."

CHAPTER EIGHT

UNLESS YOU WANT to stay the night.

Carly cringed. She couldn't believe she'd said those words out loud. Oh, she'd been thinking them. Boy, had she ever since his warm, strong hands had worked their magic on her sore, tired feet. Her entire body had responded to his foot massage.

But asking Jake to spend the night here?

He'd already spent the night before, she reminded herself.

But not with her.

I promise I'll be careful.

So much for keeping that promise. She gulped.

"You want me to stay the night," he said, his steady tone the exact opposite of the way her insides trembled.

Carly noticed he hadn't asked a question. Was he that sure of himself? Or of her? She didn't like thinking she was so transparent. She was no longer the immature teenager who wore her heart on her sleeve. Maybe it was time to remind them both of that. She sat straighter.

"If you want to." Carly wanted a cue from him to tell her she wasn't making a big mistake. "Being here might make things easier in the morning."

"I'm all for easy."

She was afraid of that.

"I already put my presents under the tree," Jake said. "And I have a bag with extra clothes in the car."

As she thought about why he might keep extra clothes in his car, Hannah's words echoed through Carly's head.

He doesn't exactly have the best track record when it comes to relationships.

"I never know what's going to happen with OMSAR so keeping a dry set, something to wear after a mission, in the car makes sense," he continued. "Though sometimes I'm too tired to change and all I'll want is to get home."

OMSAR. Relief washed over her, but a little doubt remained. "It does. Make sense."

She sounded like an idiot. Or a thirteen-year-old with a huge crush. Maybe a combination of the two.

"There are clean sheets on Hannah and Garrett's bed if you want to sleep there," Carly said.

"I could take one of the bunks in Austin's room."

Not the words of a man burning with impatience to have sex.

Was she so out of practice she had completely misread his signals? Or was he letting her set the pace and parameters of their relationship? Not that she was even sure what they had could be called a relationship.

Why don't we let whatever happens happen?

She tried not to think of the queen bed in her room. A bed too big for one person. Especially on this cold winter's night. Right now Carly wasn't sure enough of her feelings or his to do anything.

"Whatever you want," she said finally.

Jake winked. "What I want isn't a possibility. Unless it's what you want, too."

The flash of desire in his eyes took her breath away. He made her feel as if she was exactly what he hoped to find under the Christmas tree tomorrow morning. She felt the same way about him. Tie a ribbon around him, attach a gift tag with her name on it and this would be the best Christmas ever.

What was happening to her?

When Jake was around, she forgot all about being careful and playing it safe. And yet...

He seemed to know it. Darn him.

His confidence undermined hers. She didn't know what she wanted anymore.

He put on his coat. "Be right back."

As the door closed behind him, Carly rose from the couch. She shuffled her way to the front door and stood by the window, waiting and watching.

Jake moved with the agility and grace of an athlete. The snow-covered driveway didn't slow him down. He disappeared behind the back of his SUV. A moment later, he reappeared with a dark-colored duffel bag in his hand.

So he was spending the night.

No. Big. Deal.

Too bad she saw right through the self-denial. Carly wanted to believe she'd asked him to stay for Kendall and Austin's sake, but she hadn't been thinking about the kids when she'd asked Jake to stay. She was the one who wanted him to be here. She was the one who hadn't wanted to have to say goodbye. She was the one who wasn't even ready to say good-night.

As he walked up the step, she opened the front door for him. The cold night air felt good blowing against her.

Jake crossed the threshold, his presence filling the small foyer. He removed and hung his jacket on the rack. "Thanks."

Carly closed the door. As she clicked the lock in place, she felt as if she were sealing her fate, as well.

Stop overreacting, she told herself. Her reasons for asking him no longer mattered. Sure, she might have thought she was ready for something to happen, but she'd changed her mind.

"You're going to get cold feet," Jake said. "Standing in the doorway in your socks."

His warning was too late. Carly already had cold feet. She stepped back.

Jake stared at her with a wry grin on his face. "Better watch out."

Another warning? "Why?"

"You're standing under the mistletoe."

She glanced up to see the greenery hanging above. Flushed. "I forgot it was there."

Carly should move away, but his blue eyes mesmerized her, held her transfixed to the spot where she stood.

"I didn't," he said.

"But the kids aren't here to make us kiss."

His eyes darkened to a midnight blue. "This isn't about the kids, Carly."

A beat passed. She raised her chin. "What is it about, then?"

"Tradition."

Not the answer she had hoped for. And yet... *Why don't we let whatever happens happen? Why not?*

"I for one wouldn't want to stand in the way of a time-honored tradition."

Rising on tiptoes, she kissed him on the lips. Tentatively. Softly. Expecting him to back away at any second.

But he didn't.

Instead, Jake moved his mouth over hers with such tenderness she felt totally safe and in control. She parted her lips more and slightly increased the pressure of the kiss. He did the same. Carly liked being the one who decided what came next, as if they were dancing and he was following her lead.

A loud thud sounded. Not her heart. Maybe his bag? He wove his fingers through her hair. Yes, his bag.

Each step she took to deepen the kiss, he matched until she could no longer think straight to know what she was doing. Tingles flowed from her lips to every extremity. A toe-curling kiss, most definitely, but this one also had her heart doing cartwheels and her feet wanting to float off the ground.

This was far more than a Christmas tradition, far more than a kiss between friends, but Carly didn't care. She only wanted…more.

His arms wrapped around her. She arched closer, reaching up to embrace him. As she pressed against his body, she felt the rapid beat of his heart against her chest. The scent of him surrounded her. The taste of him filled her.

Her hands splayed over his back. She ran her fingers along the contours and ridges of his muscles. So strong and all hers.

For now. That was enough. It had to be.

Suddenly, Carly felt his arm come under her knees and she was no longer touching the ground. Jake carried her, as if she weighed nothing, his lips never leaving hers for an instant. He sat on the couch with her on his lap.

The mistletoe.

They were no longer standing beneath it, but that didn't seem to matter. Thank goodness.

Jake kissed the corner of her mouth. He trailed kisses along her jaw up and nibbled on her ear, shooting sparks through her.

She held on to him, her fingers digging into his back. If he let go she would slide right off his lap. But Carly knew, in her mind and in her heart, Jake would never let her fall.

He ran his tongue along her earlobe, the light touch making her quiver with delight. Desire burned like the blood rushing through her veins. "Jake."

Her voice sounded different. The word was more a plea than anything else.

"Hmmm?"

"Kiss me again."

Slowly, almost tortuously, he expertly trailed kisses along her neck until Carly thought she would burst with pleasure. Finally he reached her mouth and pressed his lips against hers.

"Like this?" he murmured.

"Uh-huh." She could barely talk, let alone think, as sensation washed over her.

She'd never felt so overcome by a kiss. Time no longer mattered. Nothing did. All she knew or could think about was Jake. How it felt to be in his arms and kissing him.

This was what had been missing in her life.

She hadn't thought she'd wanted it, but she needed it. Badly.

The cuckoo clock sounded once.

Jake kissed her hard on the lips again, and then pulled away. His ragged breathing matched her own. He struggled to catch his breath, but never let go of her.

The way he held on to her made her feel precious and adored, a way she hadn't felt in years. A blissful euphoria surrounded her. She looked up at her friend Jake, at the man who had made her feel such passion.

The hunger in his eyes made her swallow. She'd put that look in his eyes. Her and their kiss. Make that kisses. Power and confidence blazed through her.

"I need to buy more mistletoe," he said. "And put it all over the house."

She wiggled her toes. "Sounds good to me."

"Over the bed," he teased.

Carly smiled, but her heart lurched. "That's quite a line. Have you used it before?"

Jake grinned. "Not that one. I made it up just for you."

Meaning there had been other lines, she deduced. Other women. Hannah's words came back to Carly.

He doesn't exactly have the best track record when it comes to relationships. The last thing I want is for you to be hurt.

Heat rose in her cheeks. She looked away.

"Hey—" he drew her chin back up "—don't do that."

"But I…" She glanced around the room, anything to keep from meeting his eyes. "We…"

"Let me give you the same words of wisdom someone told me once. 'Don't think about it too much.'"

"Your grandmother?" Carly asked

"Your brother." Jake's eyes softened. "When we bailed right below the Liberty Cap glacier on Rainier. I knew in my gut it was the right call, but I couldn't stop going on and on about it on our way down. Finally Nick said that to me."

"But how do you…"

"Not think about it too much?" Jake finished for her.

She nodded.

"He never told me that part."

Carly laughed. "Typical Nick."

"True." Jake ran his finger along the side of her face. Her skin felt soft beneath his calloused hands. "Though I wonder what he'd say about this."

"Does it matter?" she asked, reluctant to let the moment go even though she knew Hannah's concerns.

"I want you to be happy," he said.

Which was no answer at all, and all the answer Carly needed. She couldn't live completely in the moment as Jake did. And he wasn't offering her anything else. Not yet. Maybe not…ever?

She swallowed. "I am happy. I'm…I'm glad we're still friends."

"I will always be your friend no matter what," he said. "But I'm not going to lie and tell you I don't want to kiss you again. And more. But there's no rush."

Jake wasn't offering her any guarantees, but he did care for her. Enough not to pressure her.

Her heart overflowed with so much emotion her chest felt as if it might explode. Maybe the heart was capable of growing three sizes in a day.

"Just more mistletoe," she said lightly.

"I sure hope so."

"Thanks." She wrapped her arms around him. Jake hugged back, brushing his lips across the top of her head.

He let go and stood. "I'd rather not say goodnight, but that's what I should do. And what Nick would want me to do. So I'm going to head up to Austin's room now."

She nodded, even though a part of her wanted to tell him to stay with her. "Merry Christmas, Jake."

"Merry Christmas, Carly."

* * *

Early Christmas morning, Jake stood in the kitchen. He added cloves, allspice and cinnamon sticks to the pot of apple cider and turned on the stove. The mixture needed to simmer.

He'd been simmering all night.

Sleep hadn't come easy. Not with only a wall separating him from Carly.

The kisses last night had been great. Amazing. A real turn-on. But what he felt went beyond the kisses they'd shared. The scars of the past faded away when he was with Carly. Somehow she made all the hurt, all the regret disappear.

As the oven preheated, Jake opened the refrigerator and pulled out the egg strata dish Carly had made last night using Hannah's recipe. The sun-dried tomatoes and spinach gave the dish a festive red-and-green look perfect for Christmas morning. Even the kids liked to eat it.

Kids.

Jake thought back to when he was younger. His teenage fantasy about Carly and being a part of the Bishop family had been nothing more than a pipe dream. He'd joked about it with Nick once, and if looks could kill Jake would have been six feet under. He hadn't a clue about love or relationships back then. But Jake wasn't the same, and neither was Carly.

The two of them were good together. Damn good.

"You're up early." Carly entered the kitchen wearing a purple robe and fuzzy pink socks. He wondered what she wore under it. "What smells so good?"

"Spiced apple cider." He picked up a wooden spoon and stirred the liquid to keep from taking her in his arms and kissing. "It's tradition."

The echo of his words last night brought color to her cheeks. "Whose tradition?"

"Garrett's." Jake focused on the cider. That was better than trying to figure out what type of lingerie she did or didn't have on. "I'm going to take a Thermos of cider to the hospital."

"That's thoughtful of you."

He opened the oven door and stuck the strata inside.

Carly grinned. "Keep this up, and I may have to keep you."

That didn't sound so bad to Jake. He closed the oven door and set the timer. "Just make sure I get a little time off for good behavior."

He wasn't sure if he was joking or not. That bothered him. Jake had never felt this way about a woman before. He wasn't sure he liked it.

Carly sighed, reminding him of how she sounded last night. "This really is turning into the best Christmas ever."

That was what he was afraid of.

A half hour later, the kids ran down the stairs screaming. They stood in front of the tree in total awe and silence for about two seconds. The shrieking started up again as the kids dropped to their knees to search for their presents.

All their work the past two nights had paid off. Carly couldn't be happier. Nor could she stop laughing at the kids' antics. Thank goodness Jake had set up the video camera. Hannah and Garrett weren't going to want to miss this.

The day kept getting better. It wasn't a traditional Christmas by any means, but no one had any complaints. At the hospital, Hannah kept dabbing tears of joy from her eyes. Garrett happily drank every drop of the spiced cider. Kendall and Austin loved opening more presents with their parents. Even baby Tyler seemed to enjoy himself. Being with Jake was the icing on top for Carly.

He looked so handsome and the way his smile crinkled the corners of his eyes kept her casting sideward glances his way.

As he drove them from the hospital to the house, she sat in the passenger seat singing songs with the kids. Pretending Christmas didn't exist might have made things easier, but celebrating the holiday this year made Carly realize how much she'd missed.

She didn't want to miss anything more.

"I wish today didn't have to end," Kendall said when a commercial came over the radio.

Austin sighed. "I wish there were more waiting for us at home."

Carly looked back. "We took all the presents with us to the hospital."

"Don't forget Christmas isn't about the presents," Jake said, glancing in his rearview mirror. "Remember what you heard in church this morning."

"We know, Uncle Jake." Kendall sounded years older than nine. "But it's still nice to get gifts."

"Very nice," Austin said.

"Hey, Uncle Jake," Kendall yelled. "You missed the turn to our street."

"We're taking a little detour," he said.

Carly looked at him. "Where are we going?"

Mischief sparkled in his eyes. "It's a surprise."

Excitement overflowed from the backseat as the kids guessed their destination. Even Carly joined in.

"The hot springs at Kah-nee-ta."

"Timberline Lodge."

"The brewery."

"Good guesses," Jake said. "But none are correct."

He made a right-hand turn off the highway, and Carly knew exactly what he had in mind. "Are you sure this is a good idea?"

"Yes. They're old enough." He parked at a Sno-park near other trucks and SUVs. "Remember, it's a tradition."

"What are Sean and Denali doing here?" Austin asked.

"There's Bill and Tim with little Wyatt in a backpack," Kendall said. "And Leanne's here, too."

"The whole gang," Carly mumbled, her chest tight.

Jake nodded. "It's what Nick would have wanted."

"Does Hannah know?"

Jake nodded. "Garrett convinced her it was time. Are you okay with this?"

Carly took a deep breath. "Yes."

"Then let's go," Jake said, exiting the car.

Denali, Sean's black-and-white Siberian husky with ice-blue eyes, barked a greeting and bounded in the snow.

As Kendall and Austin told everyone about their Christmas so far, Jake removed their snow boots and winter clothing from the back of his SUV. "Put these on."

"Are we going on a hike in the snow, Uncle Jake?" Kendall asked.

"You'll see."

Leanne gave Carly clothes and boots to wear.

Once they were dressed, Sean removed two gifts, awkwardly wrapped with bows stuck haphazardly on as if he'd let Denali help. "Look what was under my tree."

"Presents," Kendall and Austin yelled.

"That's right, presents," Sean said as Denali barked. "This one is for Kendall. And this one is for Austin."

"How come they were at your house?" Austin asked.

Sean shrugged. "Open them so we can figure it out."

The kids ripped off the wrapping while the dog ran between them, trying to snatch the paper away.

Austin's mouth formed a perfect O. "Snowshoes."

"Wow." Kendall hugged hers. "They're great, but Mom always says no when Uncle Jake asks to take us snowshoeing."

Jake kneeled so he was at her eye level. "Your mom gave her permission for this outing."

Kendall brightened. "Who are they from?"

"All of us," Leanne said.

Carly wiped the corners of her eyes.

"That's right." Jake helped Kendall into her snowshoes as Sean put Austin's on his feet. "You've been here a few times before, Kendall, with all of us."

Her small forehead crinkled. "When?"

"Christmas Day since you were born," Bill answered.

"Except you weren't big enough to snowshoe," Tim said. "So your dad carried you in a pack like I've got Wyatt."

Memories, long pushed aside, rushed back to Carly. Iain had offered to carry the baby pack so Nick could walk next to Hannah, but Nick wanted to do it himself. "Your daddy was sure you would fall asleep, but unlike little Wyatt, who's already napping, you stayed awake the entire time."

"Where was I?" Austin asked.

Carly put her arm around him. "One time you were at home in your mommy's tummy. Another time you were too little." There hadn't been a next time.

"We would meet here each Christmas afternoon," Jake explained. "Put on our snowshoes and hike around the lake. It was our Christmas gift to ourselves and each other."

"But we haven't done it in a long time," Bill said.

"How come?" Kendall asked.

Leanne placed her hand on Kendall's narrow shoulder. "Because three people couldn't be with us."

No. Carly looked at each one of them. That couldn't be.

This had been the best of the Christmas traditions, one Nick started when he was in high school. The first time only four of them had gone on the hike: Nick, Jake, Carly and Iain. Each year, more people had joined in. Until six years ago.

"Hey." Austin pointed to Carly, Kendall and himself. "We're three people."

"Yes, you are," Jake said.

Carly pinned him with her gaze. "You never came back?"

"It didn't seem right, but Sean thought it was time to start the tradition up again."

She hugged Sean. "Thank you."

"I did it for purely selfish reasons," the rescue leader said. "There's only a limited amount of time I can sit on my butt on my parents' couch without going stark raving mad or drinking way too much. Now I'll be able to go back to dinner and not want to kill one of my second cousins twice removed."

Carly laughed.

"By the way—" Sean handed her a present "—this was under my tree, too."

"You didn't!" She tore off the wrapping and found a brand-new pair of snowshoes and poles. "I love them. Thanks."

Leanne hugged her. "You're going to have to spend more time here so you can use them."

"Aunt Carly's coming back next Christmas," Austin announced.

Jake looked at her with a question in his eyes. Not knowing what to say, she simply shrugged.

Sean gave a quick lesson to Kendall and Austin in the basics of snowshoeing. "It might feel funny at first having these big things on your feet, but you'll get used to them. When you walk you might sink a little into the snow, and you have to lift your foot to take the next step. Try it."

The kids did, walking awkwardly.

"This is harder than it looks," Kendall said.

Carly remembered when she'd learned. "You'll get the hang of it soon enough."

Austin quacked. "It's like having big duck feet."

Jake laughed. "Sort of."

As the kids practiced, everyone strapped on their snowshoes. The way people joked and laughed the way they always had warmed Carly's heart.

"Where's Austin?" Tim asked.

"He's right…" She looked around, but didn't see him. "Austin."

No answer. Her heart dropped to her feet. As everyone called Austin's name, Bill studied the snowshoe tracks.

Austin popped out from behind a tree with a big grin on his face. "Gotcha."

Carly drew in a sharp breath of cold air. It was as if the ghost of Christmas past—okay, Nick—had just paid a visit.

"You got us all right," Tim said finally. "But when we're outdoors like this, it's never good to hide, buddy."

"Sorry." Austin walked over to them. "Uncle Jake taught me never to go off on my own, but I saw that tree and…"

"It's okay, dude." Sean tugged on the top of the boy's hat. "Your dad used to play jokes like that all the time."

"Really?" Austin asked.

Jake nodded. "He would always say 'gotcha' when he got us."

The boy beamed. "Like me."

Carly hugged him. "Exactly like you."

"Cool," he said. "Can I practice some more?"

"Go ahead," Sean said. "But stay close."

As Kendall and Austin practiced getting the hang of walking in snowshoes, Jake rubbed the back of his neck. "That was…"

"Eerie," Tim said.

"No kidding," Bill added. "The way he said 'gotcha' gave me chills."

Carly crossed her arms over her chest and rubbed them. "I got shivers."

"Me, too," Leanne said. "I don't think the goose bumps are going to go away anytime soon."

Jake nodded. "He sounded like Nick, an octave higher, but still…"

Sean agreed. "Total déjà vu."

"That was weird, and most likely a coincidence, but did anyone think we may have just gotten Nick's blessing for this little outing?" Leanne asked.

A breeze blew snow from the branches of a Douglas fir and onto the kids. They jumped up and down with gleeful delight. Denali barked.

Jake stared at them. "I think you're right."

The group stood. Silent. Watching. Carly couldn't help but think of Nick and Iain, but the memories weren't sad or even bittersweet. Peace surrounded her, both inside and out. She smiled. Coming here had been the right thing to do.

"We'd better hit the trail," Leanne said. "We don't have too much light left."

"And don't forget," Bill said. "We're supposed to be home for dinner."

"Please," Sean said. "Can't we forget?"

Carly called the kids over.

Jake laughed. "No, because your mother will call the sheriff, who will put out an alert and then we'll have all of OMSAR looking for us."

Tim laughed. "And the press will be out in full force since you brought along the pup."

As if on cue Denali barked.

"Don't forget the kids," Bill added. "They would be worth a few sound bites and scathing letters to the editor from city folk who wouldn't know a carabiner from a key chain."

"Is it time to go yet?" Kendall stood at the head of the trail. The same way Nick used to do.

"It's as if Nick's right here with us," Carly mumbled.

Jake smiled at her. "Who's to say he isn't?"

CHAPTER NINE

THIS WAS SO NOT what Carly had in mind.

Her legs burned. Each breath of cold air stung. Sweat ran down her back. She struggled to put one foot in front of the other as she snowshoed along the trail.

All Carly wanted was to be alone with Jake for a few minutes and pick up where they'd left things last night. So when someone had to go back to get the Thermos of hot chocolate they'd left after a snack break, she had volunteered, leaving Kendall and Austin with the group. Carly had imagined a romantic stroll for two in a winter wonderland, not wilderness adventure racing with an outdoor Adonis.

She blew out a puff of air.

"You're doing great," Jake encouraged. "We're almost there."

Easy for him to say, he wasn't huffing and

puffing with each step. She wanted to plop down on a rock and rest for a minute. Okay, ten.

"When we get there, I want hot chocolate and cookies."

Jake grinned. "You can have whatever you want."

His suggestive tone brought a smile to her face. Maybe she'd get a kiss or two before they reached the gang.

"The kids aren't moving too fast," he added. "We'll catch up to them soon."

And maybe she wouldn't. Unless she did something about it.

She tried giving Jake a sultry look, the effect no doubt spoiled by her red face, runny nose and ducklike feet. "What if I don't want to catch up to them?"

"You can do it," he said encouragingly. "Remember the cookies."

His cluelessness knotted her spine with frustration, but she wasn't about to tell him she would prefer his kisses to cookies. Not when she'd been the one to kiss him last night. "Right."

Jake continued along the trail. Carly struggled onward.

She had been able to keep up with the guys when she'd been younger, but not anymore. Leaving the mountain meant leaving a life of

outdoor recreation behind. But even though she
was out of shape, out of practice and totally out
of her league, she'd been willing to suffer a
little indignity, a little inconvenience to be alone
with Jake. She had feelings for him, deep
feelings she wanted to explore. "What if my
legs gave out and I couldn't walk another step?
Hypothetically speaking."

"We'd stop until you could keep going."

Sultry had been a bust, so she batted her eyelashes. "You wouldn't carry me?"

He gave her a look. The look. The one her
brother had used when she wanted to wimp out
on a skiing run or hike. "Suck it up, Bishop."

Those were the same words Nick used to say
to her. And that's when it hit her. All day, Jake
had been treating her like Nick's little sister.
Not the woman he'd kissed last night. She
wanted to know why. "I need to stop."

Jake turned toward her. "Have a drink of
water. You'll feel better."

Carly drank. Physically, she felt better, but
emotionally… She shivered.

"Cold?" he asked.

"What are we doing?" she asked.

His brow creased. "We're snowshoeing."

"That's not what I mean." She tried again.
"What do you want out of this? Us, I mean."

"I want you to be happy."

She thought about his reply for a moment. "You want the kids to be happy, too."

"What's wrong with that?" he asked.

"Because I'm not a kid anymore," she said, irritated. "You alternate between wanting to devour me with kisses and treating me like Nick's little sister. I don't get this hot-and-cold treatment."

"Hot and cold?" Jake repeated.

She crossed her arms against her chest and glared at him. "How about just plain cold?"

He glared back. "You are Nick's little sister. I'm trying to be considerate here. Make you happy. What's wrong with that?"

She didn't want to argue, but Jake brought out the best and worst in her. "I know you've gone out of your way these past couple of days to make Christmas special for both the kids and me. I appreciate you and all you've done. It's been magical and wonderful. But instead of trying to give me what you think will make me happy, why don't you ask me what I really want?"

He flung his arms wide. "Okay. What do you really want?"

"I want what I thought I lost on this mountain six years ago. I want what I thought I could never have again. Love. A happily ever after. And I think I want it with you."

Jake stood silent. A beat passed. And another, while her hands and feet turned icy cold and apprehension froze her chest.

"I want you, Carly," he said finally.

A little warmth trickled through her. That was good. But it wasn't enough. "But do you want to have a relationship with me or just a fling? Which is it, Jake?"

Her question hung in the icy air.

"There you guys are!" The call came down the trail.

"Hot chocolate!" Kendall cried.

Jake's eyes met Carly's in unspoken apology as the group came down and surrounded them.

Or was that relief?

Do you want to have a relationship with me or just a fling?

Carly's question had been on Jake's mind ever since they got back from snowshoeing. And he still didn't have an answer for her or himself.

Outside, he placed the garbage bag into the can. His breath fogged in the cold night air, but he wasn't in a rush to go indoors. The kids were in bed. That would leave him and Carly alone.

Jake secured the top on the garbage can.

He'd always gone for what he wanted. The

only time he hadn't was with Carly. First, she'd been too young. Then she'd fallen in love with Iain. And then there had always been Nick, who would have punched Jake out for thinking about his little sister that way. Even after Iain and Nick had died, Jake had hesitated to act on what he wanted because of Carly's grief and his own guilt. Those had all been good, valid reasons, but now… Now nothing stood in the way.

I want what I thought I could never have again. Love. A happily ever after. And I think I want it with you.

Nothing but him.

Jake wanted only the best for Carly, but he didn't know if he could give her what she wanted. He didn't know if he could be who she wanted.

He walked slowly to the back door, shoving his bare hands in his pockets. No matter what he decided, Jake had one thing left to do, one more thing to offer her. He entered the mudroom and made his way to the kitchen.

"Let It Snow" played on the radio. Carly dried her hands at the sink. She shot him a strained smile, her unanswered question still hanging between them. "The dishes are loaded. The only thing left is straightening the living room."

Jake's work was almost done here. Almost.

She walked into the living room, kneeled beside the Christmas tree and arranged the toys underneath. "It's hard to believe Christmas is over."

Jake leaned against the couch, watching her. "There's still a few hours left."

Carly got a wistful look in her eyes. "I guess."

He walked over to the tree. "Christmas can't be over because I haven't given you your present."

"You got me the snowshoes."

"Those were from all of us." Jake reached under the red-and-green velvet tree skirt and pulled out a gift he'd hidden two days ago. "This is from me."

Whatever else he could or couldn't give her, he could give her this.

She stared at the package, wrapped in bright red paper and tied with a white ribbon. "You didn't—"

"Open it," he urged.

Carly looked at him with hope and doubt before turning her attention to untying the lopsided bow and unwrapping the box. She removed the top of the box, unfolded the white tissue paper and stared at the front of the photo album made from wood. She ran her fingers along the stained and polished cover. "It's beautiful, Jake."

"You told me by looking back you could move forward," he explained. "I thought this might help."

She opened the first page and gasped. "This is from when we were kids."

"Hannah has all the pictures organized so that made them easy to find." Jake couldn't tell if she liked it or not. "The beginning of the album is filled with my favorite pictures of us. All of us. The rest of the book is blank so you can fill them as you make new memories."

Tears welled in her eyes. She blinked.

Carly thumbed through the pages, laughing and wiping her eyes at the all those times spent together, all those long-forgotten memories...

Jake got a funny feeling in his stomach that spread throughout his entire body and seemed to settle in his heart.

"Do you remember this one?" She pointed to a picture of her, Iain, Nick and Jake climbing at Smith Rock. "Or this one, when you and Nick took me backpacking?"

He laughed. "How could I forget the huckleberry ice cream incident or the run-in with Mr. Skunk?"

How could he forget any of this?

Jake had been dragging his feet, afraid to commit his life to Carly, but she was already part of his life. The proof was right in front of him. All those pictures of them. The good times and the bad. Sure, there was a six-year gap, but now that she was back, Jake knew exactly what he wanted. He wanted to be in the rest of the pictures. He wanted to fill all those blank pages with memories of the two of them. Together.

"This is incredible," Carly said.

No kidding.

"Thank you." She closed the album and looked up at him, her eyes shining. "It's the best gift ever. Well, next to the dog sled ride."

She laughed. So did he. Happy, relieved, nervous.

Jake hadn't felt so alive, so whole in six years. He felt as if he was starting all over again. As if his heart was brand-new, full of wonder and waiting for new discoveries. As if this woman sitting next to him was all that mattered, and would ever matter to him.

Carly parted her lips slightly. He took that as an invitation, pressing his lips against hers. Warm, soft, smooth.

Now this was the perfect Christmas present.

Moving his mouth over hers, he reveled in

the taste—a mix of spices, chocolate, Carly. Exotic, sweet, unique.

And all his.

Finally.

Jake wrapped his arms around her and pulled her closer. He wanted to make the most of the moment.

No more "should have."

No more "what if."

No more regret.

He kissed her, holding nothing back. As his lips savored every sensation, heat sizzled through his veins.

She arched toward him, never removing his lips from hers. "Oh, Jake."

Her eagerness thrilled him. Turned him on. He combed through her hair with his hand, his fingers twisting in the silky strands.

He wanted…more. Okay, her. And for the first time, he had the chance he'd dreamed about all those years ago.

But this had nothing to do with then, and everything to do with now. He'd finally found home, where he belonged, and he wasn't ready to let go.

Jake didn't know if this was the best thing for Carly, but it was what he could give her. That had to count for something.

He kissed her as if she were the moon, earth and sun. And right now she was all three. The past, the present and, he hoped, the future.

His mouth moved against hers, wanting her to know how he felt. Words wouldn't do. He wouldn't know what to say or how to say it, but this kiss…

Yes, this kiss.

Hear me, Carly. Jake deepened the kiss yet again. *Please hear what my kisses are saying to you.*

Carly didn't want Jake to stop kissing her. Not now, possibly not ever. That fact alone should have sent off warning bells, but all she wanted was more kisses.

He had one arm around her back and his other hand in her hair. She scooted closer until she was on top of his lap.

For so long, she'd felt alone. But no longer. Carly wasn't alone. She didn't have to be alone ever again.

As he kissed her neck, she sighed.

Carly didn't want this to stop. She didn't want to let Jake go.

Don't think about it too much.

She focused on the now. On Jake's kiss. How his lips caressed her, showered her with love.

Don't stop.

"I'm not planning to."

Carly must have said the words aloud. She didn't know. She didn't care. No one had ever kissed her so thoroughly, so intensely. And...

Crying.

She stiffened, a nanosecond before he pulled away from her. "One of the kids."

Jake swore and then sighed. "Let's go."

Her swollen, bruised lips longed for more kisses, but she knew where her responsibilities lay. So did Jake. She crawled off his lap and stood. He laced his fingers with hers.

Carly smiled. She climbed the stairs with Jake at her side. The crying came from Austin's room. She pushed open the door.

"Austin," she said softly.

The boy sobbed from the lower bunk bed. "I miss my mommy."

"Aww." Carly pulled him into her arms. "It's hard when you miss your mommy and she's not here."

Austin hiccupped. Jake kneeled at the side of the bed. "Your mom will be home soon, buddy."

Austin sniffled. "I want her home now."

"I know you do." Carly combed her fingers through his short, tangled hair. "But she needs to be in the hospital right now to recover from having Tyler."

"What if she never comes back?" Austin asked.

Carly didn't know how to answer. He might not remember his biological father, but he knew his daddy had left one day and never come back. "Your mommy loves you very much. No matter where you are or where she is."

"Your mom wants nothing more than to come back and be with you," Jake added. "But she has to wait until the doctor says it's okay."

Austin wiped his eyes.

"Do you want to call her?" Carly asked. "Would that make you feel better?"

"What if the baby's asleep and Mommy, too?" Austin asked, sounding like a caring, considerate big brother. Nick would have been so proud. "That wouldn't be good to wake them up."

"She wouldn't mind," Carly explained. "She doesn't want you to be sad."

Austin looked at her. "I won't be sad if you sleep with me."

"That bed's a little small for two," Jake said.

Austin brightened. "I could sleep in Aunt Carly's room."

"Can I sleep there, too?" Kendall asked from the doorway.

Carly gave Jake a rueful look. The regret in his eyes matched her own.

He touched her shoulder. "It's okay."

His understanding touched her heart. This wasn't what either of them wanted, but they had no choice. She looked at the kids. "If you want to sleep in my bed, that's okay."

Austin jumped out of bed and grabbed his pillow.

"I'll go get my stuff," Kendall said before disappearing.

Carly glanced up at Jake. "I'm so sorry. I didn't think things tonight would end like this."

"Hey, no worries," he said. "We have plenty of time to be together."

Together.

The thought sent a burst of heat rushing through her veins. Anticipation built within her. "I can't wait."

He smoothed her hair with his hand. "You won't have to wait long."

She took a deep, satisfied breath.

"Go crawl in bed with them," Jake said. "I'll make sure everything's turned off and lock up before I go."

"You could stay—"

"I can't." He gave her a quick peck on the cheek. "But I'll be back tomorrow."

"Aunt Carly," a high-pitched voice call-ed out.

"I better go," she said. "Thank you."

"For what?" he asked.

"For being you." Carly smiled. "And making this the best Christmas ever."

Jake grinned. "Just wait until next year."

CHAPTER TEN

THE NEXT MORNING, the doorbell rang. Kendall and Austin ran to the front door, their footsteps shaking the ornaments on the Christmas tree.

"Don't open the door until I get there," Carly said, padding her way from the kitchen.

"It's Uncle Jake," Austin shouted.

Her pulse quickened. "Go ahead then."

"Good morning." Jake stepped inside, for a moment his gaze met hers, then he closed the door behind him. He handed Austin a pink box. "Here you go."

Kendall peeked inside. "Donuts."

"Don't open the box until you're in the kitchen," Carly said as the kids skipped off, giggling the entire way. She felt like giggling herself.

Jake's hair looked damp and his face baby-smooth, as if he'd recently showered and shaved. Carly fought the urge to reach out and touch his face. There would be time for that.

"Thanks for the donuts," she said. "Much tastier than what I had in—"

He kissed her on the lips, hard and fast, taking her breath away and tripling her heart rate in seconds.

Jake pulled his left arm from behind him and handed her a beautiful bouquet of mixed flowers. "These are for you."

Her lips tingled from his kiss, her heart from his thoughtfulness.

"I didn't know what your favorite flower was," he admitted.

"These are." Carly took the bouquet and sniffed the colorful blossoms. A sweet floral aroma filled her nostrils.

"Which ones?"

Happiness swelled inside her. "All of them."

Jake winked. "Today's my lucky day."

"You might be right about that." She stared at the flowers. "But I thought you only brought flowers to dates and hospital visits."

"This could be considered a date."

Contentment settled over the center of her chest. "You think?"

He nodded. "Of course we have chaperones, but Hannah and Garrett should be home later today."

Excitement surged. Not that Carly didn't like being with the kids or didn't want to help out with Tyler, but she really wanted a little alone time with Jake. Okay, a lot of time, but she would take what she could get. "I know."

"I can't wait to steal you away."

"I'm yours for the taking."

"Promise?"

She laughed. "But don't forget, I'm still here to help Hannah."

"I've got you covered."

"How?"

"Leanne will come over to help Hannah with the kids so I can take you out."

Carly glanced at the cuckoo clock. "How did you manage to arrange help at eight o'clock in the morning?"

"My methods are top secret," he whispered, his breath hot against her neck. "I'd tell you, but then I'd have to kiss you."

"I wouldn't mind."

"Me, either." He peered around her shoulder. "But our audience might have something to say about it."

She glanced behind her. The kids stood in the doorway to the kitchen. Austin had chocolate icing smeared all over his face. "We'll be right there."

The kids didn't move.

Carly sighed. No rush, she reminded herself. Besides she needed to put the flowers in water. "Come on, let's eat breakfast so we can make gingerbread."

Standing in the kitchen, Carly inhaled deeply. "Okay, that's it! Everybody outside."

"Why?" Kendall demanded.

"The gingerbread needs time to cool," Carly said.

Jake's eyes met hers, still with that delicious warmth in his gaze. "I need to cool off, too," he murmured, too low for the kids to hear.

Enough of his accidental brushes and subtle on-purpose touches had Carly agreeing with him.

Everyone put on their coats, hats and gloves, headed to the front yard and made a snow family to welcome the baby.

As snowflakes drifted down from the sky, Carly wrapped a multicolored striped knit scarf around a snowwoman's neck. "What do you think?"

Kendall beamed. "It's perfect."

Things were perfect. Especially with Jake.

Carly smiled, feeling warm inside even though snow fell from the sky. She couldn't wait until it was just the two of them.

Soon, she told herself. Very soon.

A pager beeped. A cell phone rang. Jake checked both. "Excuse me for a minute."

He took the call, but didn't speak. He didn't have to for Carly to know who was on the other end. She could see it in his eyes, had seen that similiar rush of adrenaline when a call came summoning Nick for a mission.

Jake would be heading up to Mount Hood for a rescue. She glanced in the direction of the summit, but couldn't see it. The weather must be bad up there.

She wrapped her arms around her stomach to fight the sudden chills and quell the knots forming in her belly.

He put his phone in his pocket. "That was a call-out for a mission. There's a briefing at Timberline."

"Cool," Austin said then returned to his snowman. Kendall didn't seem the least bit interested.

Jake nodded.

"You're excited about this." Carly had been through this enough times with Nick to know how pumped these guys got at the thought of heading up the mountain, but she had never worried that much about her brother. Sure, Carly might have felt an inkling of concern and told him to be careful, but she had never been afraid.

Not the way she was now.

"I'm not excited someone's in trouble, but I like getting out there," Jake admitted. "We all do."

"The weather has to be bad up there."

He shrugged. "Nothing we haven't faced before."

Maybe him. But not her. She hadn't faced anything like this before. Worry consumed her entire body. And she didn't like it.

A heaviness pressed down on her, threatening to overwhelm her. She felt as if a keg of beer had been laid on each of her shoulders, making it impossible for her to move or do anything. Was this how Hannah had felt each time Nick went out?

Carly didn't want Jake up on the mountain today. Not any day. Her chest constricted. "Do you have to go?"

He checked his pager again. "Yes."

The single word spoke volumes. She took a deep breath to calm her nerves. It didn't help. "When do you have to leave?"

"Soon."

Something flashed in his eyes. He meant…now.

Her heart pounded in her ears. A snowball-size lump lodged in her throat. She hadn't felt like this since…

Iain and Nick.

The kids hugged Jake goodbye. They laughed and smiled as if he were driving to the store to buy ice cream, not climb a mountain in whiteout conditions to find people who had lost their way or been injured. Or died.

The pit of dread deep down in her stomach made her nauseous. Carly thought she might be physically ill.

"Take care of your Aunt Carly while I'm away," Jake said to the kids.

"We will," Kendall said.

Austin nodded. "Promise."

"Thanks." Jake kissed each of their foreheads. "Now run inside and see if the gingerbread has cooled."

The kids ran up the porch stairs and into the house. The front door slammed close.

Tears stung Carly's eyes, but she wasn't about to cry in front of him. She'd climbed enough with Iain to know Jake needed his full attention on what he was about to face. Nothing else could be on his mind. Especially not her.

Jake walked to her, his long strides putting him at her side in seconds. He cupped her face with his hand. "You've lost your smile."

She forced the corners of her mouth up. "It's still there."

He touched her lips with his fingertip. "Don't worry."

The tenderness in his eyes was nearly her undoing. She looked up at the gray sky.

"Worrying won't bring me back sooner, Carly. It'll just make you miserable."

"How can I not worry?" she asked. "And don't you dare tell me to try not to think about it too much."

He grinned. "I won't now."

Carly couldn't believe he was smiling and sounded so lighthearted. She pressed her lips together.

"Remember, we're trained for this. We know what we're doing." Jake held her hand and walked to his SUV. "But things usually take longer up there than you think they would."

Those were not the words she wanted to hear.

"As soon as I'm finished, I'll come back here."

"If you come back," she muttered.

"Oh, I'm coming back." He kissed her long and hard on the lips. She clung to him, afraid to let go, but he backed away. "You won't be able to get rid of me that easily."

"Promise?" she asked.

He brushed his lips across hers once more. "Promise."

She wanted to believe him. "Be careful. And safe."

Jake gave her a quick hug. "Always."

She wanted to reach out and touch him one more time, but he was opening his car door and sliding inside.

"See you later," he said.

Carly sure hoped so.

Excitement buzzed in the cafeteria at the Wy'East day lodge. The scent of coffee lingered in the air. Packs and poles rested against the walls. Duffel bags and jackets lay on the tables. The lousy acoustics made voices louder and echo through the large room.

As unit members talked about the past week, Christmas with their families, ice-climbing jaunts and skiing escapades, Jake sat at one of the tables and listened. For the first time, he had more in common with the first group, the family guys, than the other two.

Times were changing, he realized. For the better.

Sean sat next to him and handed him a coffee. "Just the way you like it, Porter, strong and hot." .

"Thanks." Jake took a swig, needing both the jolt of caffeine and the warm liquid. The twenty-eight-degree temperature would make for a cold slog, but a break in the snowfall an hour ago and the resulting improvement in visibility would help. As one of the older, longtime unit members had told Jake during one of his first missions, it could be better, but it could be a helluva lot worse.

Sheriff's Deputy Will Townsend entered the cafeteria. He was the county sheriff's office's SAR coordinator. Jake had climbed with him several times and knew the deputy would shed his uniform and head out with the rescuers if he could.

Alan Marks, the incident commander, or the IC, followed. The IC was an OMSAR member who interfaced with the sheriff's office and kept everyone informed of what was going on out there. The IC cleared his throat. Unit members at the tables and those standing around quieted.

"Hope everyone had a nice holiday," the IC said. "The subject is a thirty-seven-year-old male, Samuel Sprague from Portland. He's an avid hiker who received new snowshoes for

Christmas. He wanted to try out his present and see how high he could get on Mount Hood. The subject was last seen heading up climbers' right on the Palmer snowfield. He called his wife at ten o'clock this morning saying he was lost, and due to the conditions, couldn't tell where or how high up he was. We are working to pinpoint the position of his call. Attempts at further contact have been unsuccessful."

The guy had the sense to call for help, but that didn't mean he knew what he was doing out there or would stay put until someone came and got him. If he did move, Jake knew that during whiteout conditions people unfamiliar with the mountain usually followed the fall line down until they ended up in Zig Zag canyon. Not a fun place to be with the snow and cold temperatures if you weren't prepared and carrying the right equipment. But depending on which way the guy headed or how high he'd gotten, he could also be on the White River Glacier. Or anywhere else in between.

"The subject is carrying a pack, but he didn't fill out a permit so we don't know what supplies he's got with him," the IC continued. "We do know he doesn't have a GPS or MLU with him."

Sean looked at Jake with a raised brow. No

doubt he was probably thinking the same thing. The use of Mountain Locator Units in winter had been a heated topic for a couple of years.

"The logical assumption would be he stayed put after calling his wife and is waiting to be extracted, but we all know logic doesn't always play out in these situations," the IC said. "The team leaders know their assignments. Good luck and be safe out there."

She hoped Jake was safe out there.

Carly tried to keep herself busy so she wouldn't think about him so much. She helped the kids make a gingerbread house and decorate gingerbread cookies. They played games until Hannah, Garrett and Tyler arrived home. The fuss over the baby kept Carly occupied. So did making dinner.

"Ready to call it a night?" Garrett asked after helping her with the dishes.

"I want a cup of coffee," Carly said.

"You won't sleep," Garrett warned as he went upstairs to help Hannah with the baby.

Forget being kept awake, Carly couldn't sleep. Not with Jake up the mountain.

Horrible what-if worst-case scenarios played out in her mind. A few real ones, too. She'd grown up on this mountain. She knew what could happen up there. She'd experienced it firsthand.

A car drove by on the street, the tires crunching on the snow and ice. Carly waited for the car to stop, prayed the car would pull into the driveway, but it kept going.

Not Jake.

Waiting for the coffee to brew, she remembered the last time the clock had moved this slowly. Carly prayed tonight wouldn't end up the same.

Hannah walked into the kitchen with the water bottle the hospital had given her. A large plastic straw stuck out of the blue lid. "How are you holding up?"

"I would have brought you water. You're not supposed to climb the stairs too much."

"I know, but I went very slowly. I needed to walk, and I wanted to check on you." Hannah filled the bottle with cold water from the refrigerator. "So don't try and change the subject."

"I'm…" Scared to death. "Hanging in there."

"Then you're doing better than I did when I first started dating Nick." She refilled the water bottle. "I had heard the term SAR, but knew nothing about climbing let alone mountain rescue. I didn't know what to think or how to feel. I had both my radio and television on waiting to hear some word. I couldn't believe how relieved, how happy, I felt when he called to tell me he was finished and all right."

"You were Nick's girlfriend. You had every right to be worried about him."

"So do you." Hannah smiled. "Anyone can see there's something between you and Jake."

Carly blushed. "I did try to be careful."

"I'm sure you did." Hannah gingerly lowered herself into one of the kitchen chairs. "How's it going?"

Carly picked up the tin of cookies from the counter and placed them within Hannah's reach on the table. "Everything was so wonderful until…"

"Jake headed up the mountain."

Nodding, she sat. "Now I don't know if we…if I…"

"The waiting gets easier." Hannah reached for a gingerbread man. "When I knew things were getting serious with Nick, I joined OMSAR. I did a few fund-raising events and helped out where I could, including the rescue base at Timberline. Doing that showed me what really went on during a mission. How well trained everyone was, the work that's involved and why things take so long. It almost sounds like a cliché, but they really mean what they say about keeping rescuers safe. They don't take chances with their lives. The last thing anyone wants is to increase the number of injured patients during a rescue."

Carly remembered Nick telling their parents something similar when he joined OMSAR. "I guess being there would help."

Hannah nodded. "After Kendall was born, I couldn't be at the base. That was hard because I wanted to know what was going on. I would listen to the radio and check online. I still do that during missions. Friends are out there, and family, too."

Hannah yawned.

"Go to bed," Carly said. "You should sleep when the baby sleeps."

"I don't want to leave you alone."

She forced a smile. "I feel better after talking with you."

Hannah looked doubtful.

"Really," Carly reassured.

"Okay, but let me know if you need anything."

Alone again, Carly listened to the news on the radio and heard a brief report about a missing Portland man lost snowshoeing, but no updates. She checked news Web sites and a Northwest climbing forum, but none had any new information.

She was just going to have to wait. Except…

Carly didn't want to wait. She didn't like this feeling of uncertainty, of being worried and afraid. She couldn't think straight or eat. It was exactly how she'd felt six years ago. She cringed.

What was she doing?

Carly had never wanted to experience those feelings again. Yet here she was. Her insides tied up in knots waiting to find out if Jake came back or not.

No matter how much Carly cared about him or wanted to be with him, she couldn't do this. She couldn't put herself through this over and over again, each time he went on a mission. Even if she were strong enough, which she wasn't, she didn't want to do this.

Not ever again.

Exhausted, Jake moved slowly from his SUV to the porch. Normally he couldn't wait to get home after a mission, but he hadn't even considered going there first. There was only one place he wanted to go tonight.

Scratch that.

Only one person he wanted to see.

As he climbed the front steps, the door opened. Carly stood with one hand on the doorknob. "You're back."

Damn, she was beautiful. A smile tugged on the tired corners of his mouth. "I'm back."

"How did things go up there?"

"Another team found him," Jake said. "Cold and hungry, but happy to be rescued."

"Are you hungry?" she asked.

"Starving." He kissed her on the lips. "Exactly what I needed."

She opened the door wider. "Come inside so you can warm up and get something to eat."

Jake looked down. He'd been in such a rush to get here he hadn't changed. "I'm dirty."

"You smell like the mountain."

True. All of his mountain gear and clothing had a particular scent, a mix of sweat and earth, of dirt and rock and mud—a smell that never went away. "I'll go around to the mudroom and change there."

"I'll heat up dinner for you."

Later at the kitchen table, he gobbled up the spaghetti with Italian sausage along with a salad and three slices of garlic bread.

She sat across from him. "You really were starving."

"It's not often I get a delicious home-cooked meal. Great dinner. Thanks so much."

Carly pushed the tin of cookies toward him. "You're welcome."

Jake took a one-eyed gingerbread man. He hadn't had one of these in years. "How's Tyler doing?"

"He's such a good baby." She stood and cleared his plate from the table. "Kendall and Austin aren't quite sure what to make of him since he doesn't do much right now."

"I'll wash the dishes," he offered.

"You've done enough."

He snatched another cookie. "I can handle a dirty plate."

"So can I." Carly rinsed his plate off in the sink. "And I wasn't the one out being a hero today."

"I'm not a hero."

"You saved a man's life."

"We were just doing our jobs," Jake explained. "We're not heroes."

"You volunteer. You don't have to do what you do."

"I have a skill and I'm trained to help people who need help. That's not a hero." Jake wiped his mouth with a napkin. "A hero is someone who finds themselves in an extraordinary situation and rises to the occasion like a guy driving by, stopping and pulling another person out of a burning car. That's a hero."

"I disagree." She tossed the dishrag into the

sink. "What you do makes a difference. You help people. You save lives. That's a hero in my book."

"Why are we arguing about this when I could be holding and kissing you?"

Carly leaned with her backside against the counter. He didn't like seeing the wariness on her face, the tension bracketing the corners of her mouth. "I was worried about you today. Terrified something bad might happen to you up there."

"That's normal given what you've been through."

"Normal?" Her voice cracked. "There's nothing normal about what I went through today. I never went through anything resembling this when Nick went on a mission."

Jake didn't get it. He knew he was fine. She should trust his ability to take care of himself. "What's the difference?"

"You're not my brother," she admitted. "The feelings I have for you…"

Jake grinned. "I like hearing you say you have feelings for me."

"Well, I don't like saying it." She gripped the counter with her hands. "If I didn't have feelings for you, I wouldn't care what you did. It wouldn't bother me that you risk your life for yahoos who have no idea what the ten essentials are, but go up anyway ill-prepared and un-skilled. I wouldn't care that you go after experienced, well-equipped climbers who run into really bad luck up there. I wouldn't care at all. But I do and it bothers me. A lot."

The tightness in her voice, the emotion in each word, made him realize how much she cared. He rose from the table.

"Rescuer safety is paramount in any mission. We don't put ourselves in harm's way."

"Not when you went after Nick and Iain?"

"That was different. And you know that." Jake lowered his voice so he wouldn't wake anyone upstairs. "OMSAR has said no to certain rescues when the risk level was deemed too high. We're out to assist people, not hurt ourselves."

"You're on an eleven-thousand-foot mountain, Jake. Anything could happen up there. Sure, rescuer safety is important, but you put yourself at risk for ice fall, rock fall and a whole bunch of other nasty stuff every time you go on a mission." She stared at the hardwood floor. "Don't tell me you don't."

"Look at me, Carly," he said, reaching out to her. She did, but didn't take his hand so he took hers instead. "You know me. I like a good rush as well as the next person, but I'm not some adrenaline-junkie, death-cheating thrill seeker looking for his next fix. I'm not going to take stupid chances with my life. You have to believe me."

"I want to believe you." Her words filled him with relief, and he squeezed her hand. "But today, tonight, I couldn't stop thinking about whether you were safe or not. Whether you would come back or not."

"I'm here." Jake embraced her. She felt so warm, so good in his arms. "I came back."

"This time." She sunk against him so he pulled her closer. "I want a family. I want what Hannah and Garrett have."

"You can have that, Carly." As Jake held her, he rested his chin on the top of her head. "Nothing is standing in the way. Our way."

"But something is standing in the way."

His gut tightened. "What?"

"The mountain. Mountains," she admitted. "I can't live with the uncertainty I felt today. I don't want to."

He loosened his arms and looked down at her. "I don't understand."

"You can't guarantee nothing will happen to you, that every time you're going to come back."

"No one can guarantee that," he said.

"But the odds are higher with you."

Jake felt her slipping away. He didn't want to let her go. He touched her arm. "I could see why you'd think that after what happened six years ago. But it's not like I'm climbing a big mountain route in the Himalayas or Patagonia or even Alaska. You have to understand, there are always risks no matter what people do, whether it's climbing a mountain or driving to the store."

She said nothing.

"Carly."

"I need guarantees," she said softly, backing away from him. "I need to know you're safe. I need to know you will be coming off that mountain, alive and in one piece."

"There are no guarantees. You might want them or feel you need them, but they don't exist, Carly." He moved closer to her. "Even if I never climbed again, I could still be hit by a bus. That's how life works."

"Maybe that's true, but I can't go through it again."

His heart skipped a beat. She didn't mean… She couldn't…

Jake stared at her. He expected his father to tell him to change his ways because he wasn't good enough, but Jake never thought Carly would tell him what he ought to do. He'd given her everything he thought she needed. He was ready to give her everything she wanted. But if she wanted this… "Are you asking me to stop climbing?"

"No," she said without hesitation. "You love climbing. I would never ask you to give it up."

Relief washed over him. Climbing was a way of life for him, a life based in relationships with his partners and the mountains they climbed. "Good, because I don't want to give it up. I can't give it up. But I don't get where this leaves us."

"Where we've always been. Where we should have stayed. Friends. Just friends," she said, as if everything they'd shared had never existed, as if these past few days had been nothing more than boot tracks swept away by the wind.

Jake didn't buy it. He wouldn't let her dismiss what they had so easily. Sometimes a single boot print would be scoured into the snow and preserved when the others had disappeared. He wanted to hold on to the woman who had left her mark on his heart. He didn't see why anything had to change. "What if I don't want to be just friends? Then what?"

Carly's eyes glistened. "Then I guess there's nothing left to say except good-night."

CHAPTER ELEVEN

CARLY COUNTED the lunch receipts so she could close the register. She'd been back in Philadelphia more than a week, but still didn't feel settled. She missed Hannah and the kids, missed being in Hood Hamlet, missed…Jake.

Two weeks later, his words still reverberated in her memory.

What if I don't want us to be friends? Then what?

Then nothing.

Good-night had turned into goodbye.

She hadn't seen him again. In a town the size of Hood Hamlet, that took some effort on his part. But Jake had made it clear. He hadn't wanted to be friends. He hadn't wanted anything to change between them. But she couldn't allow things to stay the same, and she couldn't change the way she felt.

And that was that. Over. Finished. The end.

She'd been trying so hard to avoid heartache again these past six years, but it had found her anyway. The hurt still felt raw. She wanted it to go away.

Brian, one of the brewery's bartenders, motioned her over to the bar. Two televisions hung from the ceiling on either side of the bar. A twenty-four-hour news channel played on one, a sports channel on the other. He handed on a tall glass of freshly brewed ice tea complete with lemon, a straw and a small purple paper umbrella. "Here you go, Carly."

"Thanks." She appreciated his efforts and took a sip, but her favorite drink didn't make her feel any better. Nothing had. She didn't think anything would. "The lunch rush takes its toll."

Brian wiped off the bar with a white towel. "So does spending nights in your office."

She stirred her drink with the straw. "Who said I'm sleeping in my office?"

"Rumor," he said. "You have to admit, you're always here."

"It's my job to be here." Better here at work than at her apartment. That place felt empty. Transitory. Lonely. After being in Hood Hamlet she'd gotten used to being around noise. People. Family. "But I may have been putting in a few extra hours this week."

Brian raised a brow. "A few?"

Ignoring him, she took another sip of her tea.

He tossed the towel under the bar.

Something on one of the television sets caught her eye. She glanced up. A picture of Mount Hood with the words *Missing Climbers* was displayed on the screen. A shiver inched down her spine. "Turn that off. No. Turn it up."

She was an idiot for watching this. The climber on the news wasn't Jake. It couldn't be. She was punishing herself needlessly because she couldn't be the woman Jake wanted her to be. The partner he deserved. But...

Brian adjusted the volume on the news channel.

"The two injured climbers spent last night on the mountain," the anchorman, who was dressed in a perfectly tailored suit with coordinating tie, said. "The deteriorating conditions have frustrated rescuers trying to reach the two men."

Jake? Fear slithered through her. No, not him. But someone she knew could be trapped on the mountain. No matter if it were a friend or a stranger, Jake would be looking for them.

Every single muscle of hers tensed. Her stomach roiled.

The news cut to a woman reporter standing outside Timberline Lodge. She looked like she was freezing to death even though she wore a blue down jacket, a matching hat and thick gloves. The swirling snow made it seem as if she were standing in the middle of a snow globe gone wild. More than once the reporter lost her balance when a gust of wind hit.

Carly's chest tightened.

If the weather was that bad at six thousand feet, it had to be a complete whiteout up top with high winds and—

"Weren't you just there?" Brian asked.

She nodded impatiently, her attention fixed on the screen. The camera panned the landscape. She recognized the lodge. The Sno-Cats. The men and women wearing OMSAR jackets with the white lettering on them. Where was Jake?

The picture returned to the studio. The news desk looked so safe, so boring compared to what had been shown on the screen before.

"But rescuers haven't given up and continue to battle the elements," the anchorman said with a polished tone and blinding white teeth. "The teams were pulled off the mountain due to high winds and whiteout conditions yesterday, but with the break in the weather this morning, they headed back up. As you can see from our live footage, the weather has begun to change again. Most rescuers are on their way down, but at least one team may bivouac, that is, spend the night on the mountain, to take advantage of another weather break."

Oh, Jake.

Rescuer safety is paramount in any mission. We don't put ourselves in harm's way.

Carly shook her head. That didn't mean he wouldn't be one of those spending the night on the mountain.

"Wow," Brian said. "I bet you're glad you're back here in civilization, huh?"

Of course she was. If Carly were there, she'd have to spend every minute glued to the news, shaking with anxiety, desperate to learn the fate of the climbers and the men and women searching for them on the mountain. Just like six years ago. Just like...

Now.

And that's when it hit her. No matter if Jake climbed or not, did mountain rescue or not, she wouldn't stop caring about him. She couldn't turn off her concern even if she lived across the country from him. Because no matter what he did or didn't, she would love him. She would always love him.

A new image appeared on the screen. The

wives of the two injured climbers stood with Deputy Townsend. With amazing composure, one of them thanked the rescuers for battling the elements to search for her husband. She mentioned her husband was in the military and had just returned home after deployment in the Middle East. He'd been counting the days until he could climb Mount Hood with his best friend from childhood.

Hearing what the soldier survived during his tour of duty only to return home and be hurt on Mount Hood seemed ironic and wrong. But Carly realized Jake had right. Guarantees didn't exist. No one could avoid risk.

Unless they wanted to avoid love altogether.

Carly had. Once. But no longer.

The warmth flowing through her pushed the coldness away. She was ready to take chances even if it meant another broken heart.

Jake.

She loved him. Nothing else mattered.

It was that simple, that complicated.

Carly slid off her bar stool. She knew exactly where she needed to be.

And with who.

The mountain takes; the mountain gives back.

As Jake carved S turns with his skis in the

powder, the cold wind stung his face. People had died on Mount Hood. Some who were lost had never been found and were part of the mountain now. It wasn't right or wrong. Just the way things worked. Which was why climbers, smart ones at least, treated the mountain with respect. No one wanted bad karma following them up there.

Today was one of the better endings. Adrenaline rushed through him. A happy ending.

Boo-ya.

The emotional high overcame his exhaustion. The team had found the two climbers, too late to bring them down safely with the weather conditions, so they'd built a snow cave and hunkered down for the night. Both men had suffered injuries from a fall, but they'd had the right gear and enough experience to survive that first night on their own. They'd been hurting, but relieved to learn they wouldn't be alone for a second one.

Fresh rescue teams had arrived early this morning to take the injured down. His team had handed off the two subjects and stuck around until the groups headed down the mountain.

Sean, who led the rescue team, swooshed down on his splitboard in front of Jake. Bill and Tim skied behind them. Just like old times. The four of them hadn't been on a team together in a while.

And like the old days, they turned down a Sno-Cat ride to the bottom. Nothing like the buzz of a successful mission to keep you going when everything else wanted to shut down. Even though they were cold and tired, not to mention hungry, no one wanted to pass up a run on new powder. Jake felt as good as a guy with a broken heart could feel.

Nearing the lodge, he saw the numerous satellite dishes sticking up. The media was out in full force on this multiday mission. No doubt the reporters would be waiting with microphones and questions.

Not that he minded.

Not when everything had turned out well. That was a welcome change from the way he'd been moping around. The last two weeks had been bad. A day hadn't gone by when he hadn't thought about Carly. Hadn't missed her. At least not until heading out on this mission, where he'd been able to push everything out of his mind, including her, and focus.

The team stopped and removed their skis and splitboard. As soon as the press noticed them, the mob with cameras, microphones and tape recorders surrounded them.

People shouted out questions. Jockeyed for position. Waited for a sound bite.

"What was it like spending the night on the mountain?"

"Did you ever think you wouldn't find them?"

"What led you to the climbers?"

"How do you feel right now?"

A knowing glance passed between Sean and Jake. Explaining to others how they felt right at the moment was nearly impossible beyond the clichéd "exhausted, excited, overwhelmed, running on adrenaline." At this moment, every-thing down here felt insignificant, almost trivial, to what they'd been doing up there.

"That's a good question for our rescue team leader to answer," Jake said.

Sean shook his head, but he was the one team leader who always had something colorful or incendiary to say. He hadn't become a media darling for nothing.

Jake would owe him a beer or three for sticking him with that though talking to the media was preferable to being left alone with thoughts of Carly hammering through his brain. Celebrating at the brewpub tonight might bring him out of his funk.

He wove his way through the crowd toward the day lodge where warm beverages and hot food awaited him. His boots crunched against the packed snow. His muscles ached. His stomach growled.

He looked at the double glass doors in front of him and nearly fell flat on his ass. It was all he could do to hold on to his skis so they didn't clatter to the ground.

"Carly?" The unexpected sight of her brought a rush of warmth. Forget about a cup of coffee, he had all he needed right here. She stood there in her bright purple jacket, black pants and snow boots, blond strands hanging out from beneath her hat, looking like a dream. Except for the worry etched on her face. "What are you doing here?"

"I saw the news." Her hazel eyes stared into his. All this time, he'd never noticed the gold flecks in them before. "I was worried, but most of all I just really missed you."

She'd dumped him.

But…she'd missed him.

Worried about him.

Jake got a grip. Yeah, and that's why she dumped him, because she didn't want to worry about him anymore.

"Let me get this straight, you dropped everything, hopped on a plane in Philadelphia and flew out here?"

She bit her lower lip. "Pretty much."

Who was he kidding? Jake rested his skis against the wall. He didn't care why Carly was here. The fact she was proved… Hell, he didn't know what it proved. He was just glad to see her.

Jake kissed her, a kiss full of need and pent-up frustration. She tasted warm and sweet. He wanted more.

Carly touched him, her hands shaking. Her arms wrapped around him, holding him, as if to assure herself he was all right.

"I stink," he said.

"I don't care."

She trembled.

"Honey, it's all right." He held on to her, holding her close to his body and his heart. "It's okay. I'm okay."

"I know." She ran her hands up his arms, cupped his face. "You're trained for this, you don't take unnecessary risks. I know. But I was still so scared."

And that's when he knew.

This wasn't okay. It wasn't worth it.

Jake followed his gut, knowing his instincts wouldn't lead him astray. He couldn't have her so worried about him all the time. He loved her too much to put her through this over and over again.

He looked down at her. The love reflected in her eyes nearly ripped his heart apart. She hadn't asked, but he knew this was what he had to do. "I'll quit mountain rescue."

Carly drew back. "What?"

"I'm not letting you go again." He ran his hand down her arm. "I won't climb again if that's what it takes to be with you."

She stared up at him, her expression full of wonder. "You'd do that? For me?"

"Whatever it takes." Jake squeezed her hand. "I love you."

"You don't have to stop climbing. The mountains are a part of who you are. I could never take that away from you." Her smile reached her eyes and touched his soul. "What you do with OMSAR is important. That doesn't mean I'll like it all the time or not worry, but I'll try not to think about it too much. As long as I'm with you, it'll be okay."

"Damn straight, it'll be okay." He picked her off the ground and kissed her. "You'll be with me."

"Yes, I will." Her eyes sparkled as he placed her on her feet. "I was afraid of taking risks, afraid of losing someone I loved again, but you taught me to take chances. I didn't know what would happen when I got on that plane yesterday. I don't know what will happen now. But I'm willing to let whatever happens happen. And I'm willing to do that with you. I love you, Jake Porter."

"Remember, I said it first."

She laughed. He kissed her again.

Two teenagers carrying snowboarders walked by and snickered. One muttered something about getting a room. Punks.

She stepped back. "As much as I'd like to continue this, you've got to be cold and hungry and wanting to get out of those boots. Let's get you inside."

"Not yet." Jake wasn't prepared, but it didn't matter. He knew this was the right time. Balancing with his pack on his back, he lowered himself to one knee and held her hand. "This hasn't been the most traditional relationship, and we haven't really had an official date yet, but I don't care. Carly Bishop, will you marry me?"

Tears slipped from her eyes as a smile lit up her pretty face. "Yes, of course I'll marry you. I want to be with you no matter where you go or what you do. Even if it means climbing the tallest peak in the world."

He stood. "Everest?"

"Whatever makes you happy."

"You make me happy, Carly." Jake pulled her against him and never wanted to let go. "It's always been you."

Celebrate 100 years
of pure reading pleasure
with Mills & Boon®

To mark our centenary, each month we're
publishing a special 100th Birthday Edition.
These celebratory editions are packed with extra
features and include a FREE bonus story.

Plus, you have the chance to enter a fabulous
monthly prize draw. See 100th Birthday Edition
books for details.

Now that's worth celebrating!

September 2008
Crazy about her Spanish Boss by Rebecca Winters
Includes FREE bonus story
Rafael's Convenient Proposal

November 2008
The Rancher's Christmas Baby
by Cathy Gillen Thacker
Includes FREE bonus story *Baby's First Christmas*

December 2008
One Magical Christmas by Carol Marinelli
Includes FREE bonus story *Emergency at Bayside*

Look for Mills & Boon® 100th Birthday Editions at
your favourite bookseller or visit
www.millsandboon.co.uk

FREE

4 BOOKS AND A SURPRISE GIFT!

We would like to take this opportunity to thank you for reading this Mills & Boon® book by offering you the chance to take FOUR more specially selected titles from the Romance series absolutely FREE! We're also making this offer to introduce you to the benefits of the Mills & Boon® Book Club—

- ★ **FREE home delivery**
- ★ **FREE gifts and competitions**
- ★ **FREE monthly Newsletter**
- ★ **Books available before they're in the shops**
- ★ **Exclusive Mills & Boon® Book Club offers**

Accepting these FREE books and gift places you under no obligation to buy; you may cancel at any time, even after receiving your free shipment. Simply complete your details below and return the entire page to the address below. You don't even need a stamp!

YES! Please send me 4 free Romance books and a surprise gift. I understand that unless you hear from me, I will receive 6 superb new titles every month for just £2.99 each, postage and packing free. I am under no obligation to purchase any books and may cancel my subscription at any time. The free books and gift will be mine to keep in any case.

N8ZEE

Ms/Mrs/Miss/Mr...Initials ....
BLOCK CAPITALS PLEASE

Surname ....

Address ....

....

....Postcode ....

Send this whole page to:
The Mills & Boon Book Club, FREEPOST CN81, Croydon, CR9 3WZ